For my family, friends, and students, past and future.

Table of Contents

1

Nightmares

"Hurry, he's getting closer! There, NOOOOOO—!"

A massive earthquake erupted through the room, dropping chunks of ceiling and wall around shaken figures. Struggling to his feet, a man took position by the door, gleaming sword in one hand and steadying himself against the crumbling wall with the other. Maddening screeches filled the room, and a cowering figure in the corner looked out from behind his cloak to see hundreds of bats swarm in from the rolling black clouds where the ceiling once stood. Through the chaos, a lone, white-bearded man stood with his arms raised in front of the crib of a bawling infant, seeming to take no notice of the collapsing room.

"Pairton, finish NOW!" cried the man by the door, madly waving his sword and shielding his face as he made his way to a woman wedged into what remained of a corner.

The old man continued to ignore the flying beasts as he appeared to chant. His fingertips began to glow and a blinding beam of light filled the dark.

"Master, the door," wailed the hooded figure in the corner.

The oak door shattered, rocketing splinters across the room. With his eyes closed, the old man reached with one hand and touched the warrior's shoulder. Holding the crying child's head with his other hand, his fingertips beamed with a radiant light that sent queer shadows dancing all around. With a final flash, the shadows were quickly engulfed in darkness again.

"TENII, GO!" screamed the shaky voice of the old man as he clung to the warrior and fell to one knee.

An earsplitting explosion destroyed what was left of the crumbled walls. Through the smoke and dust, a dark figure casually emerged, cloaked entirely in black, with a hood covering his lowered head and surrounded with an eerie halo of orange light. With a flip of his arm, the cloak fell to the ground, revealing piercing red eyes, and a dark grin filled his pale face.

"NO!" cried the warrior, clinging to the side of the woman, now trembling beneath the empty crib.

"PENGADESH IS MINE!!!!"

"NOOOOO!"

Soaked with sweat, Dantin shot up and fought to catch his breath as his heart slammed through his chest. Pushing his hair behind his ears he began to calm as mumbles rose around the dark room.

"What's going on in here?" boomed an angry voice from the hallway. The bedroom door burst open, blinding Dantin with the sudden light, and a large woman in a nightgown stormed in.

"It's Dantin again," grumbled a nasty voice from across the room. "He's lost it."

"I-It's n-nothing, Ms. Mullin," Dantin squeaked, squinting and shielding his eyes with a hand against the light. "I-I just had a bad dream."

After surveying the room, her reddened eyes stopped on Dantin, shooting a foul glare right through him.

"That's it, you little devil, I've had it!" she roared, stomping over and grabbing his arm.

"E-Eleven years—" she stuttered. "Eleven years I've had to put up with you and your crazy dreams and troublemaking, I've had it. No more!" She ripped him from his bed and toward the door.

"Bye, Dantin," gloated the nasty voice from across the room. "Pleasant dreams."

"B-but, Ms. Mullin," Dantin pleaded as she half dragged, half carried his small body down the hallway. "I didn't do any—"

"Quiet!" she barked with a fierce glow in her eyes.

At the other end of the hallway she opened the door to a little room used for storage. The foldout bed was still set up from the last time Dantin "acted up."

"Get in there!" she growled as she forced him on to the bed. "And if I hear another peep out of you, you'll sleep outside in the dog house; that's where you belong anyway."

With that, she slammed the door shut, leaving him in total darkness again. Slumping back onto the bed, he cursed the old woman, wondering how his life could get any worse. Trouble found him no matter what he did. Just that very night, he had been sitting quietly at dinner when Tommy, another boy living in the home and the owner of the nasty voice from the bedroom, splattered his face with mashed potatoes. But Ms. Mullin turned around a second too late and scolded Dantin for being too messy.

One chilly autumn night eleven years ago, Ms. Mullin opened the door of the Zeta house, a group home for delinquent and abandoned children, to two City of Philadelphia police officers carrying an odd-looking infant with bright red hair and humongous pointed ears. The baby had been abandoned in the park. The only clue to his identity was a gold medallion around his neck that read *Dantin.* When no parents turned up, he became a permanent resident.

Ms. Mullin always told him stories about how he would keep everybody awake all night with his constant crying. She even got so angry one night that she told him that his parents probably left him in the park because they couldn't stand the sound of him anymore. Her nasty moods and cruel words were commonplace in the home, and Dantin was one of her favorite targets, so he'd learned over the years to deal with it. He actually learned that if he could get her *really* mad, she'd twitch, start speaking strange words no one would understand, and storm away before her face turned purple and exploded. Whenever he'd start to feel bad, he'd remember all the nasty things she's said to him and he'd sit back and enjoy the few moments of peace.

Dantin couldn't remember anything about his family, and none of the social workers who were always hanging around the house were any help. His memory seemed to be linked to the nightmares he always had, but he couldn't figure those out either. This latest one had been the worst yet. Normally, he would get bits and pieces of the dream, but he could never understand any words. He often pictured the crying woman cowering over the baby. Even through her horror-filled face, Dantin was stunned by her long, shiny black hair, pushed behind pointed ears like his own. Her complexion was perfect, beautifully white, like newly fallen snow. He guessed that in a different situation, her smile and eyes would brighten the darkest room, but the image of fear in her eyes was haunting. The man with the sword always stood proud and his powerful muscles strained as he gripped his sword and waited, but the fear and urgency in his voice scared Dantin as well.

The old man with the long, white beard was also an image Dantin could not get out of his head. He stood tall, straightening a crooked back, and chanted weird words to the dark sky. The eerie glow from the tip of his fingers gave him a warm feeling, even after the dream was over. This was the first time he had heard the booming voice. Just thinking about it made the hair on the back of his neck stand up straight and sent cold chills throughout his body. He wished he knew what the dreams meant. When Ms. Mullin forced him to talk to the guidance counselor at school, the counselor simply mumbled a few words to himself and took strange notes. He told Dantin that he had some sort of psycho-osis, or something he couldn't understand. His only suggestions were to sleep better and think of positive things before he fell asleep. Dantin rolled his eyes and agreed, wondering what he could possibly think of that was positive.

Shaking his head and trying to forget the entire night, Dantin buried his head in the pillow and fought back tears. He wished he knew who his parents were and why they had left him in such a horrible place. He lost the struggle and wept softly until he finally fell asleep again.

The next morning Dantin awoke in the same windowless closet he had fallen asleep in. Slamming his shin on a shelf as he felt for the door, he bit his lip and struggled not to cry out. As he entered the hallway shaking his head, he did not find the usual crowd of boys rushing to get ready for school. Confused, he went downstairs and found Ms. Mullin cleaning up a messy table.

"What are you doing here still?" she asked coldly. "Why aren't you at school?"

Again a cold chill traveled through his body and ended at the tips of his bare toes.

"Uh, n-nobody woke me up."

"Well, you'd better get your puny rear end out of here," she replied curtly. "School starts in five minutes, and if you're late again the principal said he would give you detention for the next month."

Dantin tore back up the stairs and grabbed his shoes and bag. He passed a mirror on the way and took a quick look. Staring back at him was a boy much shorter than the other boys his age with bright red hair that went in every direction, except straight. He was still wearing the tattered green shirt and torn jeans he had worn the day before and the first two socks he found didn't even match. Sighing, he quickly ran his hand through the bird's nest on top of his head in a feeble attempt to straighten it. Pushing it down to cover his ears the best he could, he stole one more look with sad eyes and flew back down the stairs and out the door before Ms. Mullin could yell about his messy appearance.

Being late for school was one thing Dantin was really good at. Usually, Tommy and his two henchmen, Martin and Bruno, found some way to make sure he'd be late. Once, they hid his backpack in the shower. Dantin looked for the bag for twenty minutes before he found it, completely soaked, with all his homework ruined. Mr. Mandible, his fifth grade teacher, made him scrub whiteboards during recess for a week. But Tommy wasn't really smart enough to think of creative stuff every day, so usually, Martin and Bruno just held him down while Tommy beat on him. Luckily they were already gone, so he didn't have to worry about them this morning. Yet no matter what he told the secretaries in the office, they treated him as if he were lying and sent him on his way without a pass. Dantin made the mistake one time of asking Ms. Mullin for an excuse. She started laughing so hard that he had to run out of the house because he knew he would get blamed if she laughed herself to death.

One thing that did save him from time to time was his running. He could run like the wind, which saved him from all kinds of trouble.

Martin and Bruno were big, but they were also dumb and very slow. A lot of times he could distract them and run away, and they didn't have a chance from there. Dantin was the fastest boy in the school, probably the fastest boy in any school. When he took off, you could feel the wind rush by like a speeding train.

But today, he had three minutes to make the usual ten-minute trip to school. Racing down the sidewalk, he racked his brain to come up with an excuse that would keep him out of detention. They would never believe that the perfect Ms. Mullin *actually* forgot to wake him up. With the school coming into sight, Dantin looked at his watch and saw that he had thirty seconds to make it. He tore up the long concrete stairs in front of the school as if they were a super-speed escalator, but as he opened the front door, the bell rang the new day in.

With a sunken heart, he leaned against the wall to catch his breath until a nasty voice boomed in behind him.

"Hey kid, get to class," scolded an elderly janitor from around the corner. It was Mr. Gilespe, the only person in the world meaner than Ms. Mullin. Some of the rumors say that he used to be a teacher until they found out he was beating students up for their lunch money, so they made him a janitor instead. Others tell the story of his forbidden office where he keeps the kids he captures until he sells them as slaves. He was a creepy old man with long hair on one side combed over and covering about half of his humongous, bald head and a lazy eye probably injured wrestling a first grader.

"Sorry, Mr. Gilespe, I'm on my way," Dantin panted between breaths, sticking out his tongue when the janitor looked away.

"Well, you'd better get on your way," he grumbled, "before I decide to take you for some milk money."

Dantin sped his way down the hall to the office, leaving the janitor with a barely audible comment about smelling like rotten onions. As he entered the room, the secretary looked up at him and sighed.

"Late again, huh Dantin?" she began. "What was it this time, a sudden rainstorm in your bedroom, or did you rescue three babies from a burning car accident again?"

"No, I-I must have overslept," he answered, overcoming the urge to tell the secretary that Ms. Mullin had gotten stuck in the bathtub and he had to call the fire department to bring the Jaws-of-Life. He always had interesting stories to tell the secretary, but lately, they had gotten him into more trouble than he wanted to deal with.

"Well," she said without looking up again. "The principal is in a meeting right now, so go to class and he'll be sure to call you down later."

Dantin's heart sank even further. There was only one thing worse than being scolded by the principal: being called out of class by the loudspeaker to be scolded by the principal.

"Yes, ma'am," he mumbled as he turned around and left the office. Wondering what else would go wrong, he made his way to his classroom and opened the door.

"Good morning, Mr. Smith. Glad to see you could make it," Mr. Mandible greeted sarcastically. "Is there *any* reason you're late again?"

Dantin felt a surge of heat throughout his body every time Mr. Mandible called him "Mr. Smith." Smith was the last name given to Dantin by the Department of Welfare. He knew that it was not his real name, but Mr. Mandible insisted on calling him by it every time he was in trouble, which was about ten times a day.

"I bet the wind got a hold of his ears and flew him across town," Tommy blurted bringing the whole class to laughter. "I thought I saw him flying above us on the way to school, right, guys?" he asked turning to Martin and Bruno.

"Uh—" Bruno answered, looking to Martin. "I didn't know he could fly."

"Yeah, me either," Martin followed scratching his head. "He doesn't even have wings or a cape like Superman."

"Never mind," Mr. Mandible continued, rolling his eyes. "Dantin, put your things away and get out your social studies homework. I'll deal with your tardy later."

Dantin tried to make his way back to his seat without too much disruption, but when he reached for his homework, his heart sank yet again, this time through the floor and into the basement. Instead of his homework and pencils, he pulled out smelly shorts and a bright orange shirt that almost matched his hair. He'd grabbed his gym clothes instead of his school bag. He made his way to his desk and hoped that Mr. Mandible wouldn't see him without his book, but he knew in the back of his mind that today he wasn't going to get away with anything.

"Dantin," Tommy began when he saw Dantin had no books, "do you think I could borrow your social studies book for a minute?"

"Uh-Uh," Dantin stuttered, searching for something to say.

"You *DO* have it, don't you, Dantin?" Tommy continued.

"Mr. Smith," Mr. Mandible interrupted with a disappointed voice, "would you be kind enough to come up to my desk for a moment?"

Amidst the snickers and laughter of the rest of the class, Dantin zigzagged his way through the desks, knowing that his wonderful day was about to get better.

"Where is your homework, Mr. Smith," Mr. Mandible asked flatly.

"I-I don't have it, sir," Dantin answered in a timid voice, again ignoring the thousands of sarcastic responses that were swimming around his head.

"Well, that's too bad, isn't it, Mr. Smith? What am I going to do with you now? How can I teach you if you won't even bother to do the work?"

"Well, if you *could* really teach...."

"What was that?"

"I-I said that you couldn't teach me."

"That's right, I can't," Mr. Mandible came back, raising his voice as if he had just scored a victory. "Go back to your seat and put your head down. I'll figure out what to do with you later. As it is now, you just failed your tenth homework assignment this term. You'll be lucky to even go to seventh grade."

With his heart as low as it could possibly go, Dantin returned to his desk with a slow shuffle and his eyes buried as deep as his heart. He was really not a bad student. Actually, he was one of the smartest boys in the class. Every night he was the first to finish his homework, but it rarely got to school without Tommy or his thugs getting to it. After he finished his homework each night, he spent most of his time reading fantasy books. His favorites were stories about kings and queens, witches and warlocks, and knights in shining armor. He often fantasized that he was the hero of all the books he read. He used to practice sword fighting with a stick against the fence in the back yard, but he got tired of Ms. Mullin scolding him for chipping the paint. In his dreams, he was a fantastic swordsman fighting epic battles every time he closed his eyes. He even wrote a story once about defeating a snarling beast with four heads named *Mandible* with a slice from his sword, but his efforts were rewarded with another "F" and another visit to the counselor's office. Slowly shaking his head again and laying it down on his desk, Dantin again slipped off into fantasyland where he was the king and nobody bothered him.

Aside from the normal, everyday comments from Tommy and the rest of his classmates giving him a hard time, the rest of the morning went by uneventfully. Mr. Mandible made him sit with his head down the whole time. At recess, Mr. Mandible made him sit on the picnic table next to the yard and watch the other kids play kickball. This was actually no different than any other day. The other kids never let him play. He got to play once, and he completely controlled the game, running the bases faster than any other kid and running down balls he should have never gotten to. The rest of that day he received all kinds of nasty notes telling him off, even from the nice kids in the class.

So sitting there in the sun, Dantin read a book that he had forgotten in his desk the day before. It was his favorite book in the world. It was about a little boy who became the king of a distant land and all his adventures. Dantin had probably read this book twenty times, but each time he liked it better than the last. He got so engrossed that he didn't hear the bell calling him back to class.

—THUMP

A kickball to the side of the head awoke Dantin from his trance.

"Hey, psycho!" Tommy howled from across the yard. "It's time for lunch."

Mr. Mandible simply shook his head and led the class into the lunchroom. Rubbing his throbbing head, Dantin came to yet another awful realization. He left the house without breakfast, and he was in such a hurry, he had forgotten his lunch as well. Ms. Mullin was probably rejoicing. Any time she got to eat extra food, she would dance in the streets. He made his way to the end of the line and even kind of hoped that maybe he would starve to death before the end of the school day.

After lunch, Dantin finally got the dreaded call to the principal's office, again along with the taunting and laughter of his classmates that Mr. Mandible made no attempt to stop. As he opened the door to the office, he considered making a run for it. But the only place he had to go was back home, and he'd rather see the principal than interrupt Ms. Mullin during her afternoon soap operas.

"Go on in, Dantin," the secretary said shaking her head. "Mr. Hector is expecting you."

Mr. Hector used to like Dantin. He was also the coach of the little league baseball team, and he knew how athletic Dantin was. Dantin was on the team for two weeks and he was by far the best player the team had ever seen. The only problem was that Tommy and his thugs were on the team as well, and they didn't like Dantin getting all of the attention. For two weeks they ambushed him everywhere he turned. He would come out of the shower to find his towel stolen and his clothes sitting in the toilets. Finally he had enough of it and quit. Mr. Hector had not spoken to him kindly since.

"Ahh, Mr. Smith," Mr. Hector greeted in a patronizing voice. "How are you doing today?"

"Well, I'm doing great, sir," Dantin responded with an equal amount of sarcasm. "How are you doing?"

Losing his fake smile, Mr. Hector opened a thick file sitting on the top of his desk.

"My secretary has informed me that you were late yet again. Is there another problem that I am not aware of?"

"No, sir," Dantin said smiling. "Everything is peachy."

"Glad to hear it," Mr. Hector said, playing along. "But Mr. Mandible seems to think otherwise. He informed me that you have failed to turn your homework in once again. Care to explain that one?"

Now it was Dantin's turn to let the fake smile fade. He hoped that Mr. Mandible had not gotten to Mr. Hector yet, but he should have realized that telling on Dantin was probably the highlight of his boring little day.

Mr. Hector! Mr. Hector! Dantin visualized, almost smiling. *Dantin didn't do his homework again,* **and** *he came in late,* **and** *he smarted off,* **and** *he slept with his head on the desk all morning.*

"Dantin, getting to school on time helps you learn responsibility, it lets you..."

Mr. Hector droned on in his usual speech. Continually nodding, but ignoring him, Dantin began to think of how he was going to get back to the house. He had to take a different route every day so the thugs would not get a hold of him. He was actually comforted by the fact that he did not have his bag. When Mr. Mandible excused the class, he could make directly for the door and sprint home while Tommy was getting his books together. Again almost smiling as he listened to Mr. Hector drone on, he thought that at least something would go right today.

"...and being responsible and fulfilling the tasks that are given to you are the most important things in life." Mr. Hector finished and sat back with his hands behind his head.

"I'm assigning you detention before school for the rest of the week," he continued after a moment of silence. "Maybe coming early will teach how to get here on time."

"Yes, sir." Dantin stood up straight and over exaggerated a nod and look of determination filled his face. "Anything to teach me some discipline."

"You're dismissed," Mr. Hector directed, sighing and shaking his head.

Overcoming the urge to salute, Dantin exited, smiling as his day began to look up. If he had to get to school early, he could get up before Tommy and the thugs and maybe he could even get his homework there without event. Dantin's heart rose out of the basement and took its place back in his chest. He happily walked back to the classroom thinking everything was going to work out. But he celebrated too soon.

He returned to Mr. Mandible's room during the last period of the day. He was still in a pretty good mood, even though he had to put his head down again. When the bell rang out the end of the day, he jumped up and sped toward the door. Just as he opened it, two steps from freedom, he heard the last words that he wanted to hear.

"Mr. Smith," Mr. Mandible called from behind his desk, "can I have a few words with you?"

With hopes of an easy walk home crushed, Dantin turned around and made his way back to the teacher's desk. His heart once again crashed through the basement and was making its way toward the core of the Earth.

"Yes, sir?"

"Wait until the rest of the class leaves," Mr. Mandible began, "I need to talk to you for a few minutes."

"You're not going to make me wash your car again, are you?" he said loud enough for the kids around him to hear.

"Mr. Smith!"

"Sorry," Dantin lied, watching the rest of the class leave.

"Dantin," Tommy said with a wink, "I'll see you soon." Laughing sneakily, he and his henchmen left the room and made for the exit.

After all the students left, Mr. Mandible began.

"Mr. Smith, I hope tomorrow we can have a better day. You have to learn to be more responsible, when you're given a task..."

Mr. Mandible droned on with the same speech just given to him by Mr. Hector. He and Mr. Hector must have taken the same class on how to give long, boring speeches. It was probably under the heading of "Torture" in the teaching handbook. Fifteen minutes later when he finally quit talking, he asked a question that required the right answer.

"So, did you learn anything from the little episode we had today?"

"Yes," Dantin answered with fake enthusiasm. "I learned to be more responsible and to tackle any task that is given to me by teachers."

"Very good," Mr. Mandible responded, leaning back against his chair with his hands behind his head as Mr. Hector had. He had a gleam in his eyes as if he'd just conquered the world. "That is a very important part of life. You can go now."

Relieved, and slightly amused, Dantin excused himself and turned toward the front door, not sure what to expect when he got outside.

2

Visitors

Poking his head out the front door, Dantin hoped that the bullies had gotten tired of waiting. With a sigh of relief, he saw the playground was completely empty. He took off down the stairs in a flash and headed to the house. He decided to take the long way; Tommy never looked for him that way. But as he sped around the corner of the building, a leg popped out in front of him, sending him sprawling face first onto the ground and knocking the wind out of him.

"Hey, Dantin," Tommy howled, stepping from the covered doorway. "Glad to see you could make it."

Dantin popped up and tried to run away, but Martin and Bruno were on him in a blink. Tommy must have told them he was hiding a sandwich in his coat, because Dantin had never seen them move so fast.

"Where do you think you're going," Bruno grunted putting him in a painful leg lock.

"Come on, guys," Dantin panted, desperately trying to regain his breath. "I don't have any food."

"Food?" Bruno said, giving Tommy a hungry look.

"Shut up, idiot," Tommy said, slapping the back of Bruno's large head. "Hold him down."

Kneeling down beside them, Tommy began rubbing his knuckles against Dantin's head.

"Do you think if I rubbed hard enough I could get all the red out?" he asked as Dantin squirmed against the death grip Bruno was putting on him.

"STOP!" Dantin cried as his head began to feel like it was on fire.

"Well, that's not very nice," Tommy said sarcastically. "Martin, get over here and cover his mouth."

Waddling over, Martin took position next to Tommy and covered Dantin's mouth with his fat hand.

Suddenly, out of nowhere, a great flash fell upon the group. Tommy howled and pulled his hand away from Dantin's head like he would a hot griddle.

"What the—" he screamed with widening eyes as he held his burning hand. The pain traveled up his arm and soon his entire body felt as if it was on fire. He fell to the ground and began rolling all over, screaming in pain.

While Martin looked confusedly at Tommy, Dantin bit his hand and sent him away cursing as well. Distracted, Bruno released his grip just enough for Dantin to squirm away, but not before Dantin gave him a stiff kick to the groin as he was pushing off. Not exactly sure what was happening, Dantin tore away faster than he had ever run, leaving the three bullies rolling around in the grass.

As he approached the house, Dantin's mind was racing between trying to figure out what the flash was and imagining what the bullies were going to do to him when they caught up with him. A few years ago, Martin punched at Dantin and missed, hitting a brick wall instead and breaking three of his own knuckles. Of course Dantin was blamed for it. Ms. Mullin scolded him horribly and made him do all of Martin's chores. For the next six weeks, Dantin received daily knocks in the back of his head from the cast covering Martin's hand.

Trying to shake the nasty thoughts from his head, he sighed, and walked through the front door into something he never expected.

"Dantin, come in here," Ms. Mullin called curtly from her office as he headed for the stairs.

"Yes, Ms. Mullin," he answered as he cautiously entered the room. Ms. Mullin's office was a lot like the principal's office at school. The boys were not allowed in there, and if they were called in, it was never for a snack and a nice chat.

"Have a seat, Dantin," she said, not looking up from her paperwork. Dantin noticed that she had his file in front of her. The papers bulged and the small file folder was easily three inches thick.

Dantin sat in the chair in front of her desk and anxiously waited for her to talk. After five minutes, she finally put her pen down and looked up.

"Dantin," she began, leaning back in her large leather chair. "Last night's incident put me over the top. You have been a constant nuisance since the first day you came here. I also got a call from your principal." Dantin's blood ran cold. "It seems as though you had some problems today, and he is at the end of his rope as well. You care to explain what happened?"

"Well, ma'am," he began, "after you didn't wake me up in time, I—"

"After *I* didn't wake you up?" she blurted out. Her face grew beet red and the little vein in the middle of her forehead began to throb.

"Listen here, you little devil," she said, getting angrier with every second. "If *you* had not kept everyone up all night with your shenanigans, I would not have had to put *you* in the closet. I can't baby you all your life. You need to be more responsible and take on tasks…."

Dantin sighed and ran his hand through his hair as Ms. Mullin angrily went through the entire speech he'd already heard twice that day. The longer she lectured, the angrier she seemed to get. But as she neared the end she calmed herself down and gave Dantin the biggest surprise of his short life.

"You know what?" she said, interrupting herself, relaxing and smiling for probably the first time ever. "It doesn't even matter anymore. I made some phone calls today and you'll be leaving us."

"Leave you?" Dantin said with false sadness. "But you're like my mother."

"Yeah, sure," she said, rolling her eyes. "A friend of mine named Sergeant O'Mally runs a boot camp on the other side of the state. They take delinquents like you and beat them into shape. I talked to him and he agreed to take you. Not that it will matter, you'll be in jail sooner than later."

Dantin's heart finally emerged again, but in the middle of the ocean, all the way on the other side of the world. Instead of being beat up every day by Tommy and his thugs, he'd be beat up by trained adults. He'd heard about places like this. Kids would spend up to two years there. They had to sleep in tents and they did millions of push-ups every day while listening to counselors scream their ears off. He would choose having to put up with Ms. Mullin every day for the rest of his life over going to this new place.

"They'll be coming for you first thing in the morning. Go upstairs and pack your things, and if I find anything missing, I'll report you to the police."

With that, she lowered her head again and picked up her pen. Shocked and with millions of thoughts swimming around in his head, Dantin rose out of his seat. Ms. Mullin pretended as if he was never there. She probably pretended that the last eleven years never existed. Dantin trudged up the stairs toward his closet. He no longer thought about his empty stomach. He didn't even care if Tommy and his crew came bursting through the door right now and beat the tar out of him. Nothing really seemed to matter. The next day he would be shipped away to another placement, if at all possible, the only other placement that could be worse than this one.

He plopped down on his bed in the darkness, found a book he could escape into, and was asleep in a few minutes. But the sleep didn't last long.

"Got you, you little worm," Tommy sneered, jumping on top of him and holding him down. Martin held his legs, and Bruno tied a rag over his mouth.

"I don't know how you did that earlier," Tommy growled. "But you're gonna pay for it."

The thugs flipped him over on his stomach and pulled out some rope. They tied his arms and his legs together so tight, he couldn't move an inch.

"The old crow said you're leaving tomorrow," Tommy whispered. Dantin could feel his warm breath and bits of spittle hitting his ear as Tommy spoke close. "We decided to give you a little going away present."

—Pummff

Tommy stood up and kicked him in the stomach. Dantin's muffled scream filled the room, and he felt himself slipping into unconsciousness. Bruno gave the ropes a final tug and the bullies left him there, half-conscious on the bed. Again Dantin was left alone in the complete darkness as his breath left him and he passed out.

"Your Majesty, Your Majesty, wake up," called a voice in the darkness. Dantin's eyes fluttered open and he groaned as he strained to see through the darkness. The invisible visitor pulled the gag from his mouth.

"HELP! HELP! SOMBODY HELP ME!" he screamed, thinking Tommy had come back for another round.

Unable to calm him, the figure chanted a few quiet words and with a bright flash, Dantin felt his lips glue shut.

"Oh, Your Majesty, I-I'm sorry," he cried in a hoarse whisper. "I never get that spell right. Actually, you're luckier than that boy you were wrestling earlier. I only tried to freeze him so you could escape, but I accidentally sent him a burning curse. Poor boy, it's a good thing I stopped it before he turned to ashes."

The strange figure held up his finger and it lit up like a candle

"My name is Tenii, son of Pairton, Your Majesty." In front of him, Dantin saw a short, plump man with a rough, wrinkled face, partially hidden behind a brown beard that reached to his midsection. He was only about four feet tall, but had extraordinarily long arms. "I am a life-long servant of the true king of Pangadesh, Fintabi, your father."

Not sure whether he was dreaming or was dead, Dantin stared in bewilderment. This Tenii looked like a weirdo character from a bad movie. After a few seconds he shook himself free from the daze and struggled against the bonds on his hands and feet.

"Be still, Your Majesty," Tenii attempted to calm. "You are in no danger."

Unable to either free himself or wake himself up, Dantin did his best to relax and let the dream run its course.

"Your Majesty," Tenii said in a soothing voice, "do not be scared,

I am here to retrieve you. I'm sorry about your mouth, I only tried to cover it again, but I messed up the spell and bound your lips with super-strength glue," he said sheepishly. "Don't worry, I'll figure out how to reverse it. But for now, just listen and I will tell you a story.

"Many years ago, the land of Pangadesh was ruled by a great king named Tanupa. King Tanupa was a kind ruler, but very powerful. He was loved and respected by everyone in the kingdom and had few enemies in the lands around him. His beautiful wife, Pandera, gave him two strong boys named Fintabi and Sarpene. Fintabi was the older of the two and inherited many of his father's greatest qualities for leadership and strength. Sarpene was much smaller in stature, but what he lacked in size and strength, he more than made up with intelligence.

"As they were growing up, Fintabi, the obvious favorite of the two sons, studied side by side with his father and learned how to be a fair and powerful king. He was trained by the best warriors in the kingdom in the art of war. From the elves, he learned how to use the hidden gifts nature and the forest provide. The dwarves taught him about metalwork and the crafting of magnificent weapons. The more he learned and grew, the greater he became and the more love Tanupa bestowed upon him.

"Sarpene, on the other hand, was not taught to be a warrior. The king instead wished him to be an advisor to his brother, so he studied with Pairton, my father, and the most powerful wizard in the world. His aptitude and intelligence allowed him to excel at the art of wizardry where most other men fell short. He and I studied side by side with my father for many years and we both learned a great deal about magic. Through the years, Sarpene easily surpassed my own powers and abilities and he never grew tired of taunting and teasing me about it. You see, I am only a half-blood wizard. Of course my father is full blood, but he fell in love with a dwarf, my mother, so my skills are sort of—clumsy."

Hesitating, Tenii blushed and lowered his eyes. "That is also how I explain my queer appearance," he said, reaching down and almost touching his hairy feet without bending his knees.

"Anyway," he continued, "over the years, Fintabi and Tanupa

became closer, and Sarpene grew more jealous and dark. He became more and more cruel to people around him, and took much of his anger out on me. He knew he would never be king and hated Fintabi because he would be. Eventually, Pairton began to recognize Sarpene's dark thoughts and ambitions and refused to teach him more magic. Enraged, Sarpene left the kingdom to search for someone who would teach him. Unfortunately, he found sorcerers who had been banished to faraway lands many years before. He was taught black sorcery and grew from powerful to dangerous.

"But back in Pangadesh, Sarpene was quickly forgotten and life went on peacefully. Fintabi grew into a man, and fell in love with a beautiful elf named Shanipa. They soon married and Fintabi readied himself to be king. Tanupa had grown very old and his powers had diminished through the years. One beautiful fall day, Tanupa died and Fintabi became king. The kingdom immediately loved the new king as much as they had loved the old. At the crowning ceremony, all the animals in the kingdom brought gifts. The rabbits brought fresh cakes from the land. The deer brought a special vial of water from a spring found only in the mountains thousands of miles away. King Fintabi even graciously accepted cookies brought by the skunks, though they smelled of vinegar and gagged everyone brave enough to try them. The dwarves brought him many beautifully handcrafted swords and shields and the elves brought colorful wreaths made from the freshest and most beautiful flowers, which had to be kept away from the skunks' cookies or the flowers would have wilted. The giants even sent a representative with a chunk of glacier, which was big enough to cool the castle for almost a month. Everybody rejoiced the new king and queen as they mourned the passing of the old.

"The following months were the best that anyone could remember. Eventually, it was found out that Shanipa was pregnant, and the kingdom rejoiced once again. Months later, she gave birth to a son, who they named Dantin. Immediately, anyone close to the child could see the strength in his eyes, though sometimes hidden behind a forest of fiery hair. At the ceremony celebrating the new prince, the entire kingdom came bearing gifts again, but this time the ceremony was interrupted.

"A dark cloud rolled in from the faraway mountains and covered the blue sky, blocking out the sun. Wolf packs, led by Diffamo, an evil wolf known for his brutal slayings, tore into the ceremony, scattering the crowd and killing everyone who couldn't get away fast enough. As the wolves gained control of the court, the sky grew even darker and a hooded figure appeared through a cloud of smoke.

"Knowing who was coming, King Fintabi ushered his family into the castle and locked them into the room with Pairton and me. Pairton had grown very old (212 years old to be exact), but he was still very powerful. He probably could have defeated the intruders himself, but he knew that he could not protect the royal family at the same time. So as Sarpene and his evil creatures destroyed the castle and killed the guards, Pairton called upon an ancient spell to protect the royal family. According to the spell, if Sarpene would hurt the king or queen, the powers bestowed upon each king would surpass him, the next in line until the child was old enough, and land directly on Dantin. Sarpene would lose all his royal powers and could never possess the power to rule the land.

"Pairton chanted the ancient words over the baby as Sarpene destroyed the walls around them. Just as the door bent against Sarpene's powers, Pairton finished the spell and sent the baby away with me through a hidden doorway. I escaped unseen, but the spell was too much for my father and Sarpene killed him with a few quick words and a flick from his staff. Feeling the spell still within the room, Sarpene knew the blessing my father had left on the king and queen and imprisoned them instead of killing them.

"After I escaped, I had to hide you because Sarpene would have to destroy you before he could become king. So I brought you here to live with other men. That was eleven years ago. You, Dantin, are Prince Dantin of Pangadesh. King Fintabi and Queen Shanipa are your parents and are still imprisoned. Sarpene fears that your father will die soon, so he has stepped up his efforts to find you. So I am here to retrieve you and bring you back to the kingdom."

Again lost in a daze, Dantin stared at the goofy man without moving a muscle. He even forgot about his mouth and bindings. Somehow, he believed the story and even felt the same warm tingle go through him as when the wizard blessed him.

"And now, Your Majesty, we must go," Tenii exclaimed, letting the light on his finger extinguish. With a few words Dantin did not understand, the entire room lit up as if the sun had suddenly entered. With a flash, both Dantin and Tenii vanished into midair, and the room fell again into complete darkness.

3

Pangadesh

A cheery smile filled Dantin's face as he rolled over and lay with his eyes still closed. He took a deep breath as sleep was leaving and released it with a contented sigh, wishing he could hold on just a little longer. Suddenly remembering the dream from the night before he shot straight up, expecting to find his closet. Instead, he found himself sitting in a bed of flowers softer than silk and more colorful than the brightest rainbow he'd ever seen. There were more colors within five feet of him than he even knew existed. Taking another deep breath, the fragrance of the air and flowers hit his nose and forced another smile.

Pushing himself to his feet, he scanned the area better. A short distance away was a grove of trees, full of green leaves and surrounding crystal clear pond. Glancing up and around, he watched strange birds fly through the cloudless blue sky and disappear among the leaves of the trees. The sun gave off strange warmth that seemed to go straight through him and warm him to the core, but it was accompanied by a breeze that was strong enough to cool him, yet too weak to even tussle his hair.

It felt as though he was only asleep for a minute, but the empty feeling in his stomach returned with a vengeance and he knew that it must have been much longer. His stomach began to hurt even more as he realized how long ago it had been since he'd last eaten. Getting a broader view field, Dantin turned round and round and found that he was alone.

There was no sign of Tenii anywhere. He stretched his arms to the sky and yawned, realizing for the first time his bonds were gone and his lips could open. Opening and closing his dry, sticky mouth, he decided to make his way to the pond in the middle of the trees.

As he carefully walked through the flowers and surrounding grass, his steps had a peculiar feeling to them, as if he were walking on clouds. Smiling, he bounced each step on the spongy grass all the way to the pool. As he reached the banks, he stopped again and just stared at the beauty of the sun glistening off the surface of the water and the flowers seeming to soak in each ray the same way he breathed the air. He listened to the laughter of the birds above and smiled again at the perfection of the moment. Bending down, he opened his mouth and tried to drink the pond dry. The sugary taste of the water slid down his parched throat he could actually feel tingling throughout his entire body as it reached his empty stomach. All of his limbs prickled with a warm energy. Finally stopping for air, Dantin sat up and looked around again.

The world seemed to grow even more beautiful as he leaned back against a tree and took in his surroundings again. A glowing halo seemed to surround each of the new colors and the sweet smell and cool feel of the breeze traveled through him again, relaxing him almost to the point of sleep. The edge had even been taken off his hunger. After smiling and scanning around for a few more seconds, an eerie feeling came over him. He looked around again. He had never seen anything as perfect as this meadow in his entire life. It looked as though no man had ever been there to trample a flower, cut down a tree, or dirty the water. The eerie feeling sank into his stomach as he came to a realization.

"I'm dead," he said aloud, swallowing a lump in his throat.

All of a sudden, the colors of the new world seemed to grey and the air began to smell stale. His mouth once again felt bone dry and he listened to the birds again, this time seeming to be laughing at him. Sitting down with a thud, he closed his eyes so tight he began to see weird colors of his own.

"Please let this be a dream," he called quietly to himself. "I'm not dead, please let me be sleeping."

He repeated this over and over to himself and curled up in a ball and rocked back and forth.

Suddenly a hand fell on his shoulder. Startled, Dantin jumped up and turned, stepping too close to the pool, and fell. The warm water rushed over his head. Shaking the shock from the scare and the sudden rush of water, he popped from the water and gasped for air.

"Your Majesty, it's me, Tenii," Tenii said as he reached his long arm out. "Grab my hand."

Still disoriented, Dantin grabbed the outstretched hand and Tenii pulled him to land.

"Your Majesty, I'm sorry. I didn't mean to scare you," Tenii began as Dantin tried to shake the water off.

"Tenii?" Dantin asked as the world spun around him. "What is happening to me? Am I dead?"

"No, Your Majesty," Tenii answered with a kind smile. "You are in Pangadesh."

"B-But, I though you said Pangadesh was destroyed by Sarpene?"

"Much of it was, but Pangadesh is very large. As long as you are still alive, Sarpene does not have the power to control it all. When he took over, many of your father's loyal subjects fled and ended up here. We are far away from the castle and Sarpene's control."

"Loyal subjects?" Dantin looked around confused again. "I've seen no one else but you here."

Tenii smiled and spread his arms.

"Look again. Look closely behind those trees."

Dantin followed Tenii's long, outstretched hand, and watched as hundreds of animals seemed to appear from the trees surrounding the meadow. A family of squirrels gathered on the branches of the trees. Hidden in the flowers and the tall grass, many rabbits and field mice began to emerge. A group of deer timidly poked their heads from behind the trees, but pulled them back when they saw Dantin looking at them.

"They have been watching you since I brought you here, but they are afraid. They are not sure if it is really you."

Tenii motioned for the deer to come closer. Very slowly, they started to come from behind the trees, but emerging from the pack, a young fawn raced ahead.

"Is it really you?" he asked, jumping up and down. "Prince Dantin, have you come back to save the kingdom?"

"Uh-um, I-I'm not—" Dantin stammered, not exactly sure what to say.

"Yes, Petra," Tenii nodded. "It is really him."

"WE'RE SAVED, WE'RE SAVED," the young deer exclaimed, jumping wildly through the air. "PRINCE DANTIN HAS RETURNED TO DESTROY SARPENE!"

The growing group of onlookers began to stir and throughout the crowd many "hurrahs" could be heard.

Dantin looked to Tenii for help, but Tenii was beaming just as much as the fawn. Not used to this kind of attention, he began to shuffle uncomfortably. Large crowds surrounding him usually meant he was getting beaten up. He tugged his shirt collar softly, not quite sure what to say or do. After a couple minutes of cheers, the animals began to throw questions at him from every direction.

"Where have you been?"

"What have you been doing?"

"Are you going to fight Sarpene?"

"Will you be the new king?"

"Do you have a queen?"

"Have you come to save us?"

The questions went on and on, and Dantin's head spun like a top and he began to feel nauseous. Now he knew what famous people felt like. Finally Tenii spoke up.

"His Majesty is very tired," he said, waiving his arms to quiet the crowd. "He is a little confused right now. Leave us and give the poor boy a chance to rest. This has been a very difficult day for him."

With disappointed sighs and boos, the crowd dispersed, but not before many other animals broke through to ask a few questions. Tenii shooed them away and when they were finally alone, he spoke again to Dantin.

"Your Majesty, there is much more that I have to explain to you," he started. But seeing the tired look in Dantin's eyes, he changed his mind. "But for now, you must sleep. The sleeping spell I put on you for the trip here did not exactly work as well as it should have. I have to keep working on that spell," he said with a red face.

"For now, I have a place for you to rest."

Tenii waved his hand, and a door appeared out of midair. He opened the door to a small, cozy room. Confused, Dantin looked around the door and the pool was directly behind it. But as he followed Tenii through, he looked around and saw that he was in a kitchen. Tenii closed the door and waved for him to sit down.

"Before you sleep," he began, "you must eat something."

"How about a burger?" Dantin asked as his mouth began to water and his mind pictured a big juicy slice of beef, topped with pickles, lettuce and tomatoes.

"No, Your Majesty," Tenii answered abruptly with a concerned look on his face. "We do not eat the meat of the subjects of the kingdom. They are our brothers and sisters. That is cannibalism."

"Oh," Dantin said apologetically. He lowered his eyes and tried not to think about the hundreds of hamburgers and hot dogs he had eaten over the last eleven years.

"No worries, Your Majesty," Tenii replied, again trying to comfort the concerned look on Dantin's face. "Things are much different here in Pangadesh." Without another word, he reached into the pantry and pulled out a brown chunk of something that looked like bark.

"Here, eat this, it will fill you up."

Dantin cautiously took it from him and bit off a chunk. With a surprised smile he looked at what was left in his hand.

"Strawberries and sugar," he exclaimed happily. "But it looks like bark, how did you—?"

"Never mind that now, eat the rest and I'll show you where you can sleep."

But Dantin had already scarfed it down. Tenii turned around to get another chunk, but when he turned back, Dantin had already fallen fast asleep with his head on the table.

With another kind smile, Tenii walked over and softly ran his hand over Dantin's red hair.

"Sleep, Your Majesty, sleep. When you awake, you will save the kingdom," he whispered, killing the light with a wave of his hand.

4

Gladius Aspectus

Dantin awoke again into darkness and confusion. Contemplating whether or not to open his eyes, he sighed and looked hopefully, finding himself in a darkened room. Smiling to himself, he stood up and began to investigate. Remembering falling asleep in Tenii's kitchen, he found this room to be quite different. As his eyes adjusted to the dark, he looked back at the mat he'd been sleeping on, but found no one else within the tiny room.

Noticing the peculiar decorations, Dantin stepped closer to one wall and examined a painting with three figures. He immediately recognized Tenii, standing proud next to an old, bearded man Dantin recognized from his dream. On the other side of Tenii stood a short woman with a rough, weathered face, but soft, tender eyes. Figuring it was Tenii's mother, he inspected the picture closer, straining his eyes against the dark. She had long blonde hair and a noticeable pink hue to her skin. Looking closer to her eyes, Dantin smiled to himself as he could see where Tenii got his clumsiness.

The old man in the picture indeed looked very wise. His eyes glowed with knowledge and kindness at the same time. He stood amazingly straight for a man looking as old as he did. Though his face was stern, his pride in himself and his family was evident. The realism of the painting was amazing. It almost looked like a photograph.

Tearing his eyes away from the painting, he looked toward another wall where he found a glass case with a golden sword enclosed. He moved closer and studied the intricate carvings of trees and a mountainous scene on the hilt and blade. The strong metal shone even in the dark room and looked sharp enough to cut down a small tree. He continued to solemnly stare at the beautiful sword, as if knowing how significant the sword must be and wondering why it was kept as a simple decoration. Shrugging his shoulders, he scanned the rest of the room for a way out. He found two doors on opposite sides of the room, but both were locked. Eyes widening, his heart began to thump through his chest.

"Tenii, let me out of here!" he screamed, pounding and kicking, fighting off panic.

Almost immediately he heard Tenii's concerned voice from behind the door.

"Your Majesty," Tenii called. "Are you alright?"

The door swung open and the room filled with bright light. Dantin had to shield his eyes as he backed away.

"Your Majesty, thank goodness," Tenii sighed as he looked around the room. "What happened?"

"I-I couldn't get out," Dantin stammered as his eyes adjusted. "I just couldn't get out," he repeated.

"My apologies, Your Majesty," Tenii said bowing. "Come, I will show you around."

Tenii motioned for Dantin to follow into yet another room he had not seen before. This new room was even odder than the last. It was decorated like something you would see on a Winnie the Pooh cartoon. The wooden walls were circular, like the inside of a large tree trunk, leaving room for a tiny window that let in an extraordinary amount of light. A small chair faced the bright sun, and next to it stood a wooden stand with a book and a bottle of yellow liquid that sparkled in the sunlight.

"So, Your Majesty," Tenii started, "what do you think of my home?"

"Home?" Dantin asked in a soft, thoughtful voice. He had never been anywhere he had thought of as home. Of course, he lived in the house with the other boys back at the Zeta house, but he never thought of it as home. To him, home was a place you could feel welcome and safe; a place you could go and leave all your troubles behind. Dantin suddenly began to feel warm inside. This strange place *did* feel like home. For the first time in his life, Dantin felt welcome, and safe.

"It-it's wonderful."

"Thank you, Your Majesty," the little man said, bowing again.

"*Your Majesty*," Dantin repeated sneering his nose. "Tenii, is there any way you could just call me Dantin?"

"But, Your Majesty," Tenii began uncomfortably. "I am but your servant, what right do I have to call you by your royal name?"

Dantin thought for a minute.

"But if your story is true, you have saved my life, not once, but twice. I've never heard of a servant doing that before."

"It is my duty, Your Majesty, nothing more than that," Tenii pronounced, standing up straight, but shaking his head. "I would give up my life for any member of the royal family, if that is what was asked of me."

Still unconvinced, Dantin continued.

"Then you will be my friend, not my servant. I've never had a friend before. That is what I ask of you.

Tenii's bearded face blushed as he bowed a third time. "Yes, Your Maje—young Dantin, I am your friend. And you are truly your father's son."

"But you can still save my life though, I like that part," Dantin said with a grin.

Tenii smiled and shook his head.

"Of course you do, as much trouble as you get yourself into."

The two new friends smiled at each other. Once again, Dantin was overwhelmed with warmth at the mere mention of his parents. The thought of a family was very new to him, and to have such a great family was beyond his wildest dream. He had never been treated like a person before, and he liked it. Of course, he had a few "friends" over the years, but they came and went, and mostly they just picked on him like the others. He looked at the goofy-looking little man in front of him and smiled very happily.

"So what do we do now?" Dantin asked, hoping for more of that strawberry bark. The small piece he had eaten the day before held him over well, but it was definitely time for more.

"First, young Dantin, we must eat," Tenii replied with a smile, as if he was able to read the boy's thoughts.

With a flip of his hand, the chair facing the window flipped around, knocking the bottle off the table and sending it shattering to the floor.

"Cursed chair," Tenii grumbled, producing a rag with a snap of his fingers

Dantin chuckled to himself as the little man cursed and mumbled as he cleaned it up. Dantin laughed yet again as Tenii knocked the whole table over and tripped over the chair in the process.

"Oh bother!" he proclaimed out loud, trying to fix everything. "Sit down and I will fetch us some food," he said at last, pointing to the chair and exiting.

Sinking into the chair, Dantin marveled about the softness as he seemed to sink to the floor. He reached over to the table and picked up the book. "*How to Reverse Unwanted Spells*," he read aloud. Again he laughed. It looked just like the book Mr. Mandible had been reading, *Computers for Idiots*. He flipped through the book and saw some very strange chapters.

"'How to Find Your Missing House.' 'What to Do if You Accidentally Give Someone the Plague,'" Dantin read aloud, chuckling again and not noticing Tenii return.

"Here we go," Tenii started cheerfully, but looking up, he saw Dantin reading and laughing. "Oh-um, you found my book," he said bashfully. "That's for when I, uh—you know—when spells don't go right."

Dantin laughed as Tenii uncomfortably took the book and leafed through it, moving his lips as he read.

"Here," he said, offering the open book back to Dantin.

"How to Reverse Gluing Spells," Dantin read aloud, feeling for his lips.

"Anyway," Tenii said, taking the book back and making it disappear with a snap of his fingers. "I have food for us."

"More strawberries?" Dantin asked excitedly.

"No, this is better. It's a special blend the ancient dwarves used to eat for strength and power."

"What's in it?" Dantin asked as he took what looked like the same chunk of bark he had eaten the day before.

"It's a mixture of dandelions, flour, goat's milk and ants," he explained as Dantin broke off a chunk and hungrily chewed it up.

—SHPLUUGH

"ANTS!" he coughed.

"Of course," Tenii answered, wiping the chunk of chewed-up food from his forehead. "Insects are a great source of protein."

"Insects?" Dantin repeated, using his shirt to wipe all of the taste from his tongue.

"Yes, sir, it's an old warriors' trick. Deep in the woods or on a long march, warriors will fight for the largest bugs. It's a quick source of energy. But I warn you. Don't eat the mosquitoes in the Badlands. You can never tell whose blood they're tainted with."

"I'll keep that in mind," Dantin responded, trying desperately not to think about a bug crawling around in his empty stomach. "Don't you have anything *without* insects?"

Tenii scratched his head in thought. "No, I don't think I do. Even the strawberries you liked so much were mixed with caterpillars and fly larva."

"Ughh," Dantin groaned as his stomach sank. He forgot the sweet taste and his stomach did somersaults.

"Here," Tenii said, offering a new bottle of the yellow liquid he broke earlier. "You'll like this."

"What is it?" Dantin asked, hesitantly taking the bottle.

"Not to worry, young Dantin, it's made from the nectar of buttercups."

Dantin put the bottle to his lips and took a drink.

"Shpluugh," he blurted, again leaving Tenii's face covered in spittle. *"Dishwater!"*

Tenii's eyes widened and he took a deep breath.

"Your Majesty, I'm sooooooo sorry," Tenii cried, slapping his large hand against his forehead. "The spells for dish soap and *floreus* are very close. I must have mixed them up again."

All the color had washed from Dantin's face as he slumped in the chair. Within the last five minutes he had eaten maggots and drank dish soap. He was beginning to wonder if this day would be any better than the rest. Again, his shirt came up as he desperately wiped his mouth clean.

"Here, Dantin, I'll fix it," Tenii proclaimed, chanting a few unrecognizable words and snapping his fingers. The bottle of dish soap disappeared and another reappeared in its place.

Testing the bottle to make sure it was the right mix, Tenii offered it to Dantin.

"Here you go, Dantin, this is much better."

"Are you sure you weren't just hinting for me to do your dishes?" Dantin asked as he took the bottle from Tenii's outstretched hand.

"No," Tenii smiled. "I swear on the life of the King Fintabi."

Putting the bottle to his lips once again, Dantin took the smallest of sips. The small drop filled his mouth with a buttery sugar taste, completely covering the bitter taste of soap.

"This is amazing," Dantin proclaimed, taking another drink. Within a matter of seconds, he had gulped down over half the bottle. The *floreus* warmed his body even more than the water from the stream had the day before. It seemed to flow throughout his whole body, even making his fingertips tingle.

"I'm glad you approve," said Tenii, very much pleased with himself. "It's another ancient recipe made from buttercups and—"

"Wait," Dantin interrupted. "I don't think I really want to know what's in it, do I?"

"No, Dantin," Tenii answered, laughing out loud. "Perhaps you don't."

Without another word, Dantin finished the rest of the bottle in three big gulps.

"Ahhh," he sighed, placing the bottle down and sinking back into the soft chair. The color flushed back into his face as both his hunger and his thirst were fulfilled.

"What now?" he asked lazily, hoping Tenii would say a nap.

But once again, as if reading his mind, Tenii answered differently.

"No time to rest now, Dantin, there is much to be done, and much you still need to know." Tenii snapped his fingers and another chair appeared out of midair. Tenii sat down and began to explain.

"Sarpene is holding your mother and father in the dungeons of the castle, and of course Sarpene's evil henchmen guard them day and night, and who knows what kind of evil spells also guard the room. You have to break Sarpene's control on Pangadesh and release them."

"So, how do we get to them?" Dantin asked.

"Well," Tenii began tentatively. "You must first get through the Badlands. The castle can be found directly in the middle, and every path leading to it is well guarded by creatures and enchantments. Once you get to the castle, you must find a way in. I know of many secret passages leading to the dungeons, but there is no way of knowing which passages Sarpene knows of as well. After you get—"

"Hold on," Dantin broke in. "Why do you keep saying *you*? Don't you mean *we*?"

"No, young Dantin," Tenii said, his eyes falling to his feet. "I could not go with you."

"Whoa," Dantin blurted. "You want me to do this on my *own*?"

"I am but a lowly servant with the power to do nothing but blunder simple spells. I could do nothing but hinder your advancement and place your life, and the lives of your parents, in grave danger. You *must* go alone."

"*No!* I'm just a boy, what good am I going to be against a sorcerer and his guards?"

"You will be better off without me, I can promise you," Tenii answered, not raising his eyes from the floor. "Besides, I will prepare you. You *will* be ready to face Sarpene."

"No, I-I can't, I-I won't go alone. How can I—"

"Okay, Dantin," Tenii comforted. "That is a subject for a later time. For now, there is another task for you to complete. You must retrieve Gladius Aspectus."

"Gladius Aspectus?" Dantin puzzled. "What the heck is that?"

"Gladius Aspectus, the sword of power. It is a sword that was given to your father by his father, and his father by his father and so on. It has very special powers."

"Powers?"

"Yes, powers beyond all other swords in the world."

Dantin was comforted by the thought of an all-powerful sword.

"Oh," he said remembering. "That's the sword in the glass case."

"No," Tenii shook his head. "That is my sword. Gladius Aspectus will be much more difficult to get."

"Where is it?"

"It is stored in a tower within the Badlands. Your uncle hid it away with all the other weapons and armor he collected throughout the kingdom. Our spies have located it and tell us that it is very loosely guarded."

Dantin shivered and shook his head.

"Isn't anything going to be easy here?"

"I'm afraid not."

"So what's so special about this sword anyway?"

"It's invincible."

"Invincible?"

"Yes," Tenii nodded solemnly. "Hundreds of years of battles and play have not left a scratch on the razor sharp blade," Tenii explained.

Dantin imagined all the swords he'd read about, and none of them had that kind of power.

"Well, then if it is so powerful, why doesn't Sarpene use it himself?"

"He would love to, but it has other special powers even better than invincibility."

"Like what?"

"The sword was forged from the strongest metals by my dwarf ancestors over a thousand years ago. My wizard ancestors then blessed it with a special, unbreakable spell. It cannot be used for evil purposes. The sword can sense the emotions of its user, and will not allow him to strike with anger or revenge. If his mind is filled with evil purposes, the strong blade will turn to rubber and be harmless."

"Wow," Dantin exclaimed. Ancient dwarves and wizards, how cool was this? "So how do we get it?"

"As I said, it is within the Badlands, so getting to it will not be easy. But this is definitely one task that I cannot accompany you on."

"Why not?" Dantin whined as all the excitement drained out of him.

"The wolves guarding the tower know me, and they know my scent. They will immediately notify Sarpene of my presence and all would be lost."

"What about *my* scent?" Dantin asked. "They'll tear me apart."

"That can be taken care of, young Dantin. I'll take care of your scent and you must simply outwit them."

"Outwit them?" Dantin said skeptically. "How do I do that?"

"I trust you will find a way when you get there. Until then, I must prepare you for the journey."

"But I—"

"Dantin," Tenii interrupted in a comforting voice. "You said before that I am your friend, and you were right. But I am also your servant and I care more for your life than my own. You must trust me."

"But—"

"No," Tenii sternly said. "You *must* trust me. I would not send you unprepared."

Dantin looked into the little man's comforting eyes and could see the concern. His own anxiety was eased enough for him to calmly consider the situation.

"Okay, I'll trust you," Dantin finally answered. Deep down he knew that he could trust his new friend, but that didn't untie the knots in his stomach.

"Good," Tenii smiled as he pulled the table between them.

"The tower is about a half-day's journey into the Badlands. You could get there much quicker by following the path, but it is always guarded and it is safer to journey around it."

"How will I find my way?"

"This medallion will show you," Tenii said, pulling a necklace from around his head. The silver disc attached to it shone in the light.

Dantin looked at the medallion and wrinkled his nose.

"How is that going to show me the way? It's just a hunk of metal with a man scribed on it."

"There is another one identical to it. They work somewhat like a compass works. When they are apart, each medallion will show the direction to the other."

Tenii held the medallion in his palm. It rose two inches and hovered above his hand.

"Look at the warrior pointing his finger," Tenii instructed. Dantin stared as the medallion slowly turned around and around, finally stopping with the warrior pointing at the wall.

"I have already sent spies to the tower. They left the other medallion in the room with the weapons. This medallion will show you the way. The closer you get, the faster it will spin and point."

After a few silent seconds, Dantin broke from his trance with a shake of his head.

"But if the spies know where the sword is, why didn't they just get it?" he asked.

"No, Dantin," Tenii smiled. "The only spies small enough to avoid detection are tiny birds, and they struggled simply to take the medallion."

"Once I get to the tower, how will I know which sword is the right one?"

Tenii smiled and answered. "You will know when you hold it. You will feel its power throughout your entire body."

"But I don't understand."

"Don't worry, you will understand when you hold the sword, trust me."

"Okay, but after I get the sword, how will I find my way back?"

"The tower is close enough to the edge of the Badlands that if you look closely enough at the tops of the trees, you will be able to see the light and know the direction."

"What happens if the sun goes down?"

Tenii sighed before he answered. "Then you must spend the night in the Badlands and wait for sunrise."

The thought of sleeping in the woods horrified Dantin.

"What happens if the guards find me?"

Tenii sighed and finally said, "If you are detected, there is nothing left to do but flee faster than you've ever gone before. The wolves guarding the tower will tear you to shreds if they catch you."

"T-Tear me to shreds?" Dantin gulped as all the color again rushed from his face. "I-I can't, I-I—"

"Dantin," Tenii interrupted in a soothing voice. "There is no other way. Without that sword, you stand no chance against Sarpene or his servants."

Dantin's heart sank lower than it had ever gone. He struggled to catch his breath and keep from hyperventilating. Wolves and sorcerers were the parts of his fantasy books that he did not like.

After silent moments of staring out the window, Dantin turned back to the dwarf and spoke again.

"Okay. When do I go?"

"You must leave tomorrow at dawn."

Dantin sighed, sat back in the chair, and ran his sweaty palms nervously through his mangled hair. He looked down and saw the same tattered shirt and jeans he'd been wearing for three days now. How could he fight Sarpene? He thought about all the books he had read about knights and wizards and kings and queens. The hero always had to brave the most horrible of dangers to complete his task. Dantin was beginning to realize that in this story, *he* was to be the hero.

5

Magic Marble

The rest of the day went in a blur. Dantin couldn't shake the thought of wolves tearing him to pieces as Tenii gave him more and more instructions. He felt like he was listening to one of Mr. Mandible's speeches and zoned out through most of them. The next thing he knew, he woke up in the same dark room he had the day before. He sat up and looked around, hoping in the back of his mind that the previous day had only been a dream and that Tenii would soon come in and the two of them could spend a lazy day walking around in the sun and swimming in the pond.

But smiling to himself, he knew what he had lying before him. He pushed the wolves out of his head again and went into the next room. He was surprised to look through the window and see the sun had not risen yet. Through the dim candlelight, he saw Tenii sitting in the chair, working diligently with his tongue sticking halfway out of his mouth. The little man was so engrossed in what he was doing, he did not even notice Dantin entering the room. Dantin made his way over to the chair and lightly touched Tenii on the arm.

"Aargh," Tenii yelled chomping on his tongue and knocking over the table.

"Dantin," Tenii said, amidst a few curses at his aching tongue. "I'm sorry, I didn't hear you come it."

"What are you doing?"

"It's a special spell I've been working on. In case you run into trouble."

"Trouble, huh," Dantin gulped. "What else?"

"I will explain when I finish. Here, eat."

Tenii snapped his fingers and a plate full of bark appeared, accompanied by another bottle of floreus.

"You're not trying to poison me," Dantin asked with a half smile.

"No, Dantin," Tenii answered sheepishly. "If you like, I could test it for you."

"No," Dantin said, deciding to trust his friend. "What is it?"

"Don't ask, just eat. Wash it down with the juice if you like, but you must eat. You'll need the energy."

Dantin obeyed and took a bite of the bark. It tasted like peppermint, but he still had to will himself not to think about what was in it.

"So when do I leave?" Dantin asked after he washed the first piece down with the sweet juice.

"As soon as I finish this spell," Tenii said. He began to work again. For the next ten minutes, neither said a word, besides an occasional curse under Tenii's breath. Dantin paced around the room.

"What happens if—"

"Shhh," Tenii hushed. "Dantin, please."

"Sorry."

Dantin walked to the front door and opened it into the meadow. He stared into the lightening sky, but couldn't come up with the sun over the shadowy forest. Sighing, he leaned against the frame, trying not to picture what lay within the trees.

"Done," Tenii finally said triumphantly.

Dantin closed the door with another sigh and returned to the table.

"Is that a marble?" Dantin asked, examining the silver ball.

"This, young Dantin, is a last-minute escape device. My father invented it, but it took me all night to perfect the spell. If used correctly, it could save your life."

"What if I don't use it right?" Dantin asked, still staring.

"Then it becomes very dangerous."

Dantin gulped and continued staring at the ball for a few silent seconds. How could such a small ball save his life?

"What does it do?"

"If you are cornered, and have no other possible escape route, you can throw this ball and it will stun any attackers and give you a chance to escape."

"How?" Dantin asked bewildered.

"It has a special blend of peppers that will clog the noses of all the wolves in the area. It also releases a bright flash of light that will only affect their keen eyesight. But as I said, you must be careful. They will only be stunned for a few minutes. Also, it may alert any other creatures in the area who are not close enough to be stunned."

Dantin reached out his hand and carefully examined it closer. It felt like a marble, except heavier.

"So when should I use it?"

"Only after you have retrieved the sword. If you use it before, you will not have enough time to get the sword and escape."

Dantin swallowed another lump from his throat as he pictured himself being surrounded by hungry wolves.

"Here," Tenii said, snapping his fingers. A small waist bag appeared in his hand. "Keep it in here."

As Dantin tied the pack around his waist, Tenii's hand shot out and took his arm.

"Remember," he said sternly, "only use this in great need. It may do more harm than good if you don't use it right."

Dantin nodded solemnly and carefully placed the ball in the pocket.

"Here, take some more of these too," Tenii said, handing him more bark. Dantin rolled his eyes and put the food next to the ball.

"Are you ready?"

"I-I guess so," Dantin laughed nervously, wishing that he could have said no.

"Put these on," Tenii produced a red shirt and green pants. Dantin imagined a Christmas elf as he pulled the clothes on.

"Well, the shirt's a bit large," he commented as the sleeves hung well over his hands. Looking down, he found the pants ended just below his knees, revealing his pale legs.

"They will have to do," Tenii answered, trying to hold back a chuckle.

Dantin shot him a disapproving look and pulled the sleeves up.

"Then we must go," Tenii said in a calm voice.

"Won't this bright shirt give me away in the woods?" he asked as Tenii made his way toward the door.

"No, color does not matter. The wolves are colorblind. But—" he said thoughtfully as he scratched his head. "We must do something about those shoes." With a snap of his fingers, Dantin's old, dirty shoes were replaced with furry brown slippers with pointed toes.

"Those are elf shoes. They soften your step and make less noise."

Dantin wriggled his toes around in the new shoes. They were tight, but snuggled his toes comfortably, making his feet feel light. He even bet that they would allow him to run faster.

"*Now* you are ready," Tenii said, again turning toward the door.

Dantin looked around and shook his head. Something didn't feel right, something was missing.

"The medallion," he blurted.

"Ooohhh," Tenii replied, slapping his forehead with his large hand. "Wow, without this, you'd never find your way in or out."

Dantin shot him another disapproving look as Tenii pulled the necklace from around his neck and handed it to him.

"I apologize, young Dantin," Tenii said guiltily. "I guess that I am almost as nervous as you are."

Dantin doubted that as he took the necklace and looked at the medallion. It slowly turned in his palm, but this time, the arrow pointed to the opposite wall it had the day before.

"Wait, the arrow is pointing the other way," Dantin said excitedly. He hoped that Tenii had not messed up this spell as well.

"Not to worry," Tenii said with a smile. "You'll understand once we are outside."

Dantin followed uneasily as Tenii opened the door. As they stepped out into the lightening morning, he wrinkled his nose as he looked around.

"Where are the pond and the trees from the other day," he asked.

The land looked different. Instead of the bright leaves and the silver-blue pond, he saw nothing but dew-covered grass. Off in the distance he could see a line of very dark trees.

"Don't be alarmed," Tenii said. "We're in a different spot. My house moves around."

"Oh," Dantin said, rubbing his chin. "Is that what the chapter in your book about finding your missing house is about?"

"Yes," Tenii answered as his face grew red and his eyes fell to the ground. "I misplace it from time to time. It's becomes a great nuisance sometimes."

Dantin shook his head and smiled to himself. He could picture Tenii walking around an empty field, cursing allowed as he searched for a missing house.

"Are you ready?" Tenii asked.

"I'm as ready as I'll ever be."

"Good, then let's go. Those trees that you see in the distance are the beginning of the Badlands. I can lead you to the entrance, but you are on your own after that."

As they headed off toward the woods, Dantin could see a far-off figure running toward them.

"Tenii, look," he said, pointing at the dark figure.

"Oh no," Tenii said, running his thick fingers through his matted hair.

"Is it a wolf?" Dantin asked.

"No," Tenii replied as the figure neared. "But trouble may not be far behind."

"Prince Dantin," the fawn gasped as he neared. "I've come to help."

"Petra," Tenii scolded. "What are you doing here? You know that it is not safe."

"B-but, I knew this is where you'd come," the fawn defended. "I want to help."

"No," Tenii responded sternly. "You are much too young and this is entirely too dangerous."

Dantin smiled. That same excuse had not worked for *him* the day before.

"Sarpene destroyed my family too, Tenii. Besides, I can show Prince Dantin the way to the tower," Petra pleaded.

"How do you know where he is going?" Tenii asked angrily.

"Everyone knows that Dantin is going to get Gladius Aspectus."

"Great! It's a wonder the wolves were not here to meet us as well." Tenii shook his head and scanned the edge of the woods. Dantin's eyes suddenly grew three sizes.

"Don't worry, young Dantin," Tenii soothed. "There is no way the wolves know you are coming. Petra," he said, growing stern, "go home."

"But—"

"No, Petra," Tenii said more sternly.

The fawn looked down at the ground and spun slowly. As he got a few yards away, he turned with another argument, but was quieted by Tenii again.

"Go *home*, Petra," Tenii gritted. The fawn frowned and continued on his way. Once he was out of sight, Tenii again turned and watched Dantin dance from foot to foot and run his hands through his hair.

"I'm sorry, Dantin. Are you ready?"

"Let's go," Dantin said boldly, exhaling loudly.

They turned toward the woods and walked the rest of the way without words. Dantin went over the plans in his head one more time. As they reached the edge of the woods, Tenii spoke again.

"A couple more things before you go," he said.

With a snap of his fingers and a few quiet words, Dantin felt of rush of wind and wrenched his face and coughed.

"Ugghh," he complained, gagging and turning his nose. "It smells like dead leaves and cow poop. What is it?"

"It's you," Tenii smiled. "The smell will hide your scent from the wolves. They won't be able to smell you now."

"Yeah, but I bet they'll be able to hear me puking," Dantin proclaimed, gagging again.

"You'll get used to it," Tenii said, turning his nose away as well. "You must go, the sun is almost up."

Dantin took a deep breath and turned toward the woods.

"Alright, I'm ready."

"You truly have the bravery of you father," Tenii said, beaming. "Take this as well."

Tenii produced a small dagger.

"This knife belonged to my father. It serves two purposes. It's blade is strong, but it can also be used as a key. You can put this in any keyhole, and it will unlock the door. You will need it when you reach the tower door."

Dantin solemnly took the knife and examined it. The handle was beautifully carved out of marble and the curved blade gleamed in the dim sunlight. He put the dagger in its sheath and tied it around his waist.

"What about the sword I saw in your house. It looked very powerful. Can't I take that with me too?"

"It's a great sword, but its power is far too great for you to understand. Even I cannot use it properly. My father has been the only one to use it."

"Who cares if I don't understand it? If I'm going after wolves, I want as many weapons as I can get."

"Dantin, if you don't understand the enchantments on a weapon, it may do more harm than good. Believe me, that sword has harmed me twice as much as anything I've tried to use it on."

"How?"

"That is a discussion for another time. Right now, you must go. I will be waiting right here for your return," he said, lightly placing his hand on Dantin's shoulder. "Be careful, and come back alive."

"I'll do my best," Dantin replied with a nervous smile. With that, he took off into the woods and disappeared from sight.

"Watch over him, Father," Tenii said out loud, shielding his eyes as the rising sun reached his face. "Bring him back in one piece."

6

Sacrifice

Jumping fallen logs and dodging low-hanging branches, Dantin traveled in silence. The feelings going through him were unlike anything he had felt before. He couldn't tell if he was excited or scared out of his mind. He decided that it was somewhere in the middle, but more than likely leaning toward the scared half. He made his way through the brush and traveled straight into the heart of the woods. After about ten minutes, he stopped and pulled out the medallion. Rising slowing from his palm, the medallion spun slowly, finally stopping and pointing ahead and to the right. Straining his eyes, Dantin looked through the thick brush for what lay ahead. Not noticing anything different, he put the medallion back around his neck and turned to give a quick glance back. He could still see the light of the sun in the distance, but the sky above him was growing darker and the trees were becoming larger and more dense.

It had been quite awhile since he'd heard a bird chirp or had seen a squirrel scamper up a tree. All of the nice things he'd ever remembered about forests were falling behind him as the air surrounding him seemed to grow thicker. He felt as if he could actually sense the danger looming ahead. With a sigh, he turned once more and headed off in the direction the arrow had pointed.

The next few hours went by uneventfully. Dantin continued on at a pretty good pace and surprisingly, his legs felt just as strong as they had when he began. Looking down wonderingly at his new shoes, Dantin slammed face first into a branch, knocking him to his back. Cursing aloud, Dantin rubbed his sore nose and tried to look around through watering eyes. The trees above seemed to grow together, reaching toward each other with finger-like branches, hiding the sky above. Sitting up, he shook his head and scanned around, noticing that the trees were beginning to look like a complicated labyrinth.

He pulled out the medallion again and watched as it spun quicker than he'd seen before, stopping and pointing directly ahead. Dantin's eyes grew three sizes and he dropped to his back again and tried to flatten himself as much as possible. He crawled to a large tree nearby and leaned against it, pulling out his knife and a piece of bark. Nervously chewing, he remembered reading *The Wolf Man* and pictured the snarling teeth of a wolf tearing into his flesh. Shaking the thoughts from his head, he talked himself out of turning back and cautiously peered around the tree to see what lay ahead. Way off in the distance, between some thin, sickly trees, he could just make out the dark outline of a circular building. He sat back down and had to go through the entire process of talking himself out of running away again. With another exaggerated breath, he stood and peered around the tree again to make sure he was clear to move.

—SNAP.

Eyes now growing five times their original size, Dantin froze where he stood. As his heart started beating again he looked down in horror, quite sure that anyone within half a mile could hear the rapid thumping against his chest. After a few seconds of stillness, he carefully reached for the silver ball with one hand and the dagger with the other. Standing breathlessly, he waited for whatever was approaching. Through the silence, another twig snapped and a large bush directly behind him rustled. He crouched down and hoped whatever was coming would pass over without discovering him, but knew that he could not be that lucky. Pushing his hair from his eyes and wiping his forehead, Dantin re-gripped the dagger in his moist palm. Just as he was about to throw the magical silver ball, the head of a small deer poked through the bush.

"Your Majesty," the fawn excitedly said as he emerged from the bush.

"Petra!" Dantin's face flushed somewhere between relief and anger. "What are you doing here?"

"Well, I-I kind of followed you," the fawn answered, completely emerging from the bush with a loud crunch.

"Followed me—" Dantin gasped, but then he remembered how close they were.

"Get down," he cried in an excited whisper.

Both he and Petra hit the ground at the same time. They stayed down and silent for what seemed like an eternity. Finally, Dantin thought it was safe and whispered again.

"You need to turn around and get out of here *now*!"

"But Your Majesty—"

"SHHHH!" Dantin interrupted. "Are you *trying* get us killed?"

But Dantin's warnings were too late. Off in the distance, merely fifty yards away, he heard another bush shake. His heart dropped when he realized this bush was between them and the tower. The two once again lay silently, hoping not to be discovered. But the next thing they heard sent cold chills throughout both of their bodies.

"I think it came from over here," growled a gruff voice.

Dantin's blood ran ice cold. He didn't have to guess what was coming. His mind raced as he tried to think of what to do. Suddenly, Petra did something he never expected.

"Get the sword," Petra whispered in a brave voice.

Without another word, the young fawn stood up and darted off away from Dantin and the wolf.

"Ah-ha, lunch," the wolf snarled with hungry eyes. Without a second's hesitation, he barreled after the deer.

Unsure of what was happening, Dantin watched in amazement as Petra fluidly ran through the woods, easily leaping bushes and dodging trees with little delay. But at the same time, Dantin's heart dropped when he saw the wolf do the same thing, but quicker. After both were out of sight, Dantin jumped to his feet and sprinted toward the tower, no longer caring about the noise he was making. As the tower grew in his sights, he came to another awful realization that stopped him in his tracks. The wolf had yelled to someone else. Dantin sank to a crouched position and surveyed everything around him. Sure enough, he found another guard in front of the tower door.

For the third time, Dantin had thoughts of turning back, but using Petra's actions to regain his own bravery, he slowly made his way around the back of the tower in a large circle. With every silent step he took, he thanked Tenii for the elf shoes. Small twigs that usually make a loud crack when they're stepped on made only a dull snapping sound barely audible to even Dantin. Finally he made it to the back of the tower and ran up to the wall. He stood there resting against the building, trying to think of how to get past the second guard, when he heard a sound that turned his stomach upside down and nearly brought him to his knees. Off in the distance from the direction Petra had drawn the wolf, he heard a loud yelp, followed by triumphant howling. Dantin closed his eyes and lowered his head, trying not to picture what had just happened.

But the howling served another purpose as well. The wolf standing guard in front of the door heard it and took off in the same direction. Dantin cursed him a cowardly scavenger and quickly made his way around to the now unguarded door. Just as Tenii had said, the large metal door was locked, but also just as he said, the dagger easily fit into the hole and within a few seconds of jiggling, the lock popped open. He pulled firmly and the large door creaked open just enough for him to squeeze through.

The open door let in just enough light for Dantin to see a stairway in front of him. He took the dusty steps two at a time. As he wound his way up, his stomach did some more somersaults as he pictured the wolves sharing the fresh catch. Gagging back the urge to throw up, Dantin ran head first into another large door with a loud bang. Cursing and rubbing his forehead, he felt for a keyhole. Unable to find one, he put the dagger away and pulled at the handle. The door wouldn't budge. Grunting, he pulled again with all his might. This time, the door creaked open just enough for a little light to seep through the crack. After a couple seconds of rest, he pulled again and the door budged a few more inches. After a few more tries Dantin was able to squeeze through.

He stared with a gaping mouth. A window across the round room let in enough light for him to see hundreds of swords, shields, and daggers. He looked over at the sill and saw the medallion matching his own. He picked it up and placed it around his neck, clanking it with its sister. Looking around the room, Dantin began to worry. He could see hundreds of swords, not counting however many more were hidden under the piles of shields and other objects.

"How the heck am I going to find one specific sword?" he asked aloud.

Not remembering Tenii's description, Dantin shook his head and searched the room, picking up and examining each sword he could find. He found long ones, short ones, heavy ones, light ones, swords with gleaming gems attached to the hilts, and very plain-looking ones. Then Dantin had a horrible thought. What if he brought back the wrong sword? Would he have to make the entire trip again? Dantin shook his head and tried hard not to think about it.

He continued to search for another ten minutes before he spotted a very peculiar-looking sword leaning against the wall. He stood, studying it from across the room. The hilt carried a very intricate design of twisted metal, and the sheath was decorated with small colored stones. Interested, he made his way over to the weird sword. Lifting it, he felt a tremendous surge of energy, yet the sword was as light as a wooden stick. As he pulled off the sheath, a loud, powerful scrape came through, just like the sound when knights drew their swords in the movies. The blade glowed brilliantly. He swung it above his head a few times, then made a move to stab an invisible enemy, but caught the wall instead, sending a dazzling stream of sparks to the ground. Startled, he examined the blade and saw it was unmarked. He looked toward the wall and saw a smooth line carved through, as if the cement wall had been butter. Nodding in amazement, he sheathed it and headed toward the door. Squeezing through the tight space, he hopped down the long stairway and just as he hit the bottom step, he heard voices outside the slightly opened door.

"Two miles," a rough voice grumbled. "I chased that deer for two miles before—"

"Wait," a second voice growled. "The door's open."

Dantin's blood ran ice cold. He took the last step and went toward the door, stopping and hiding behind it.

"Ooohh," one wolf whined. "Sarpene is going to *kill* us!"

"No, look," the other said. "Only one set of footprints going in. He's still inside."

The wolves crept to the door and Dantin reached for the silver ball. But as he held it up, he had a better idea. He remembered a trick he used to use to get away from Martin and Bruno. He put the ball away and took one of the medallions from around his neck. When he heard the wolves just outside the door, he threw the medallion up the stairs as far as he could. The wolves growled, burst through the door, and leaped up the stairs five at a time. Dantin waited for the perfect moment and came out from his hiding spot. He bolted out the door, slamming it shut and locking it with the dagger. Almost immediately, he heard an angry growl and a bang from the inside of the building.

"Open this door," roared an angry voice. "Open this door or I'll rip you apart."

"*Yeah,*" Dantin called out, rolling his eyes. "That *almost* convinced me."

The wolves began to howl and tear at the metal door. Dantin decided that he didn't want to meet any of their friends that may be near, so he looked around and found the direction he'd come from. Steadying himself with a deep breath, he took off. But as he ran, he could hear distant howls from outside the tower. He lowered his head and ran even faster, ducking and dodging obstacles in his way.

He continued to run as fast as he could for what seemed like an eternity, but this time he could feel his legs burn with exhaustion. Sweat poured down his forehead and stung his eyes, occasionally causing him to miss an obstacle and sending him sprawling face first. The howls continued and got closer, so Dantin decided not to take the straight path out of the woods. He began to zigzag to the right and left, hoping to throw the angry wolves off. If they could not smell him, there would be no way to track him if he didn't move in a straight line. Throughout his zigzagging, he would continually look up toward the sky, hoping it would grow lighter and tell him he was almost out. But even with his precautions, the howls continued to grow closer. Dantin dared a glance behind him and off in the distance, he could see bushes shake and he could actually hear the sound of feet trampling the ground. Unsure of what to do next, he frantically searched around for a hiding place. He could wait until the wolves passed him by, hide until morning, and make his way out when it grew light again. Then suddenly, as if an answer to his prayers, he spotted a hole between two rocks that he could squeeze into. He ran to it and squirmed through.

The hole was tight, but it was just big enough if he held his breath. He silently thanked Tenii for serving the nasty food with bugs. He'd probably lost a few pounds over the last couple days. After he was all the way in the hole, the space grew larger. He was able to turn around and even sit up. The hole let in enough light for him to look around his hiding place. It had probably been the home of some kind of a creature and Dantin hoped it would not be returning any time soon.

He waited for what seemed like an hour, but in reality was little more than a few minutes. The howls grew closer and Dantin hoped they would again move farther away, but luck was definitely one trait that Dantin knew little of. He could hear the growls and footsteps get much closer and they stopped, just outside of the hole.

"He's over here somewhere," a loud voice growled. His voice was followed by the grumblings of at least five or six others.

"Find him," an angry voice commanded. "I'm going to tear him limb from limb."

Dantin nervously tried to gulp, but his mouth had gone bone dry. He cursed his bad luck. How had the found him again? Then he came to another awful realization. He took the medallion from around his neck and held it in his palm, but he didn't even have to look, he already knew what it was doing. The medallion spun lightning quick and stopped, pointing directly out of the hole.

"Idiot," Dantin spat as he slapped his forehead. The medallion he threw had been leading them directly to him this entire time. But before he could beat himself up anymore, he heard what he had been waiting to hear this entire time.

"Look, that hole, he's probably in there."

Dantin's heart nearly beat out of his chest. This was it; he was trapped. But he did still have the sword and the dagger, but they wouldn't do him much good against a bunch of wolves. In mid-thought, he was interrupted by something squeezing its way through the hole. A second later, an angry wolf's head poked through.

"Got you!" he barked.

But Dantin was not going to go down without a fight. He pulled out the dagger and sliced down the wolf's nose. An ear-splitting howl followed as the wolf desperately backed through the hole. Dantin almost laughed at his curses and howls. Thirty seconds later, another head poked through, and the entire scene was repeated. Two more wolves did the same thing before they finally realized that it was probably not the best idea.

"Wow," Dantin said out loud. "I don't even think it would have taken Martin and Bruno as much time to figure that one out."

After some angry conversation outside the hole, one voice came through.

"You have to come out some time," he growled. "We'll be waiting for you."

Dantin's heart sank again. He looked behind him, but it was a solid wall with no holes for escape. His mind desperately raced to think of a way out. Remembering the silver ball, he got a gleam of hope. Tenii told him only to use it in extreme need, and he was pretty sure that Tenii would agree that this situation was just that. He pulled out the ball and peered out the hole. Pretty sure he could get it through, he wondered if all the wolves were close enough. Also, Dantin was a little bit worried that Tenii may have messed up the spell. With Dantin's luck, instead of stunning the wolves, it would give them super powers or something. Shaking the thought from his head he looked toward the hole. He waited until the confusion outside the hole died down a little bit and he could hear all the voices. He took aim and let go. The ball seemed to move in slow motion. It flew through the air, just missing hitting the top of the hole before it disappeared into the dim light. A second later Dantin saw a bright flash and heard blood-curdling howls from outside. He quickly squeezed back through the hole, dagger in hand, afraid of what he might find when he emerged. As he cautiously came through the opening, he could see seven wolves rolling around on the ground, growling and howling in pain.

Dantin sheathed the knife again and took off. He could just barely see a small light through the trees in the distance. He ran faster than he had ever run before. After about five minutes, he heard the howls once again.

"Great, Tenii. You don't think you could have made it stun them a little longer?" he grumbled aloud.

He ran even faster, leaping over dried-up streams and ducking hanging branches. He was too scared to get tired. He ran for a few more minutes and heard the howls getting closer again. Suddenly remembering what had gotten him caught the last time, he tore the medallion from around his neck and threw it as hard as he could in the other direction. Just by chance, it fell into a hole and disappeared from sight. Dantin continued to run toward the light. For a few minutes, he heard the angry howls growing still closer, but finally, they began to die off. But Dantin did not take any chances. He ran faster than ever and continued to do so until he could no longer feel his legs as they bounded automatically, rubberized from the effort.

His heart grew sick as he saw that the light above the trees did not get any brighter as he ran. He was instantly afraid that he would not beat the light out of the woods and would have to spend the night in this horrible place. If at all possible, he ran even faster, ignoring the fire building throughout his body.

Finally, after what seemed like days of running, he could clearly see the setting sun through the trees. The vegetation began to look greener and the air was beginning to smell sweeter. His heart lifted. Ignoring the pain throughout him, he saw the edge of the woods and a dark little figure pacing back and forth.

"TENII!"

"DANTIN!"

Dantin burst through the edge of the forest and plopped into Tenii's waiting arms.

"I-I have it," Dantin gasped, his world spinning.

"Thank heavens," Tenii proclaimed with teary eyes.

"I-I did it," Dantin said with a final gasp, passing out from exhaustion.

"I knew you could," Tenii said, laying Dantin down in the soft grass. "I *knew* you could," he repeated, as tears of joy and pride ran down his face and got lost in his scruffy beard.

7

Dreams

"Stop, boy!" echoed through Dantin's head as he tore through the woods.

—HMFFF.

The last step sent Dantin sprawling to his face. Fighting for his breath back, Dantin heard the steps slow and circle, filling the air with growls and pants.

"What's the matter, boy?" and angry voice snarled. "Too far from home?"

As air finally seeped into his lungs he flipped over and tried to scamper to his feet.

"Wait, just wait," Dantin pleaded as he was pushed down again and looked up to find four sets of sharp, yellow teeth, dripping and spraying foam with every breath.

"Tonight we dine on royalty, boys," another wolf chimed.

"Owwwwooooooooo," all four chanted together.

Frantically feeling for his sword, Dantin found his waist empty, no sword, no dagger, no marble. Millions of thoughts swam together as he found the eyes of one of the attackers, blood red without a trace of pupil.

The wolves slowly circled the boy in a taunting ceremony, knocking him back each time he tried to regain his feet. With a flicker, the head wolf's eyes gleamed as he crouched and pounced, leading the way to a royal dinner.

"NOOOOOOOOOOO!!!" Shooting into a sitting position, Dantin fought to catch his breath. Looking around, he saw that he was again in the small room in Tenii's house. Within seconds, Tenii burst through the door with Gladius Aspectus in his hand.

"Dantin! What's going on?"

Staring wide with empty eyes, Dantin struggled to understand.

"What is happening to me??!!" Dantin screamed, falling back and running his shaking hands through his hair.

"Quiet now," Tenii soothed, kneeling and rubbing the boy's sweating forehead. "You're safe here with me, I won't let anything happen to you."

As his heart began to slow, Dantin took a deep breath and opened his eyes.

"I can't do this, Tenii," he stammered. "I can't fight wolves and sorcerers. I can't get the sword. You have the wrong boy, I'm too scared. I'm too we—"

"Shhh, listen," Tenii said. "You already got the sword. You've already faced wolves and you won."

"But-but, I thought it was just a dream." Dantin again reached for his hair. "I don't know what is real anymore."

"Look at me," Tenii demanded.

Dantin opened his eyes again and looked at Tenii's weathered face.

"I'm real," Tenii said, pulling Dantin's hand to his face. "And this sword is real. I didn't go into the Badlands. *You* did."

Through the confusion, Dantin smiled and carefully pushed himself to his feet.

"Wow," he said, stretching his arms until it felt like his muscles would pull from his chest. "This pain's pretty real too."

"I bet it is," Tenii smiled, putting his long arm around the boy and leading him out of the room. "Come, let's get you some food."

"Yeah, I could handle that."

"You've got to quit waking up like that, boy," Tenii said with a sly smile as he helped Dantin ease into a chair. "You're going to give me a heart attack."

"I'm sorry," Dantin sighed as he sank into the chair. "I-I dreamt that I was being attacked by the wolves."

"No, you're safe here with me. You've been asleep for many hours, I was beginning to wonder if you'd ever wake."

"Well, I feel like I just wrestled a gorilla in the middle of running a marathon."

"Oh yeah," Tenii said with a gleam in his eye. "I can take care of that. My father taught me a spell to take care of muscle soreness. Now how did it go again…?"

"That's okay," Dantin blurted, not wanting his arms to fall off or to grow six-inch-long hairs all over his body. "I'll deal with it. But I *am* hungry enough to even eat some of that bug junk."

"Of course, that can always be arranged."

Dantin and Tenii sat around the table and ate a wonderfully tasting vanilla substance while Dantin relayed the entire story of his adventure, down to the smallest detail. When he got to the part about Petra, his eyes fell and a large lump grew in his throat.

"Petra ended up showing up, and he saved my life. But the wolves—they—"

Unable to finish, Dantin looked out the window and struggled not to cry.

"But, Dantin, Petra is fine."

"WHAT?!" Dantin blurted, searching Tenii's eyes.

"He came charging out of the woods and knocked me over. He's lucky though, he almost got a disintegrating spell put on him before I realized who it was."

"Take me to him."

The two left the house into a beautiful sunny morning. Dantin had trouble believing how such a horrid place as the Badlands could be so close to this heavenly field. But they did not have to go very far. As soon as they were spotted, they were surrounded by what seemed like every animal within a hundred miles. Dantin was again horded with hundreds of questions about the journey, and of course, Petra was the first to burst through the mob.

"Your Majesty!"

"Petra," Dantin answered with relief and excitement screaming through his veins and out of every limb.

Though the two had just met, Dantin grabbed him and hugged him as if they were brothers. Again Dantin choked back tears as he tried to thank his friend.

"I-I thought you were—" Dantin shook the thoughts from his head. "H-how did you escape?"

"Well," the fawn began, puffing out his chest as though he had conquered a hundred-foot dragon, "The wolf chased me for miles and miles. We must have been running for hours. Just when he lunged to tackle me, he stepped in a hole and went tumbling right into huge tree. After that, he must have given up because I couldn't even hear him anymore."

"I heard the scream," Dantin laughed, keeping his arm around the deer.

"So what happened?" burst from the impatient crowd. The rest of the animals again came forth with all of their questions.

"Alright, Alright," Dantin laughed, trying to quiet them down. When he finally got the animals quiet enough to hear him, he began. He too puffed out his chest and exaggerated a little bit while relaying the details of the journey. The crowd responded wonderfully with gasps, winces, and looks of astonishment. When he finally finished, it was quiet enough to have heard a bee buzzing around a flower all the way across the field.

"All praise Prince Dantin!" burst through the silence. The animals responded with hip-hip-hoorays and cheers for the boy. Dantin looked out at the field and was filled with pride. He was beginning to forget that he was only a boy and was realizing his duty and how important he was to the lives of all these animals, and all the animals and people throughout the kingdom.

"Okay, okay," Tenii finally said. "We have much work to do and not a lot of time to do it in.

"But remember," he said much more gravely, "Sarpene now knows of the prince's presence, it is very dangerous for all the animals here. He is sure to send scouts and warriors to hunt the boy, and they will not leave anyone they find alive. You must now all get away from here as quickly as possible."

The animals' faces went from excited and cheerful to dreadful and terrified. Within minutes, the entire crowd left, with the exception of Petra—Tenii could not have drug him away. The three watched all the animals run away in different directions and continued to stand in silence, unsure of what to do next.

8

Sarpene

"IDIOTS!" A fist slammed and a voice boomed throughout the dark room and echoed through the hallway, vibrating enough to stir dust and stretch cobwebs.

Three wolves cringed and slinked back with every one of their hairs standing at attention. From the shadows they could only see a fist clenched pale and glowing eyes burning holes through each of them.

"But-but, Sarpene, it wasn't our—"

"SILENCE!" In an instant, lightning shot out of the shadow and the lead wolf disappeared in a puff of smoke. Giggles came from a gnome sitting to the right of his master.

"So the famous son returns, and you fools let him walk away with a sword." The candlelight danced upon his sunken, white face as the sorcerer approached the remaining two wolves.

"Get out of my sight before you join your brainless chief," he said with a kick to the sides of each. They were gone in a flash and out of the castle before Sarpene could change his mind. "What to do, what to do?" he spoke out loud, stroking his hairless chin with long, bony fingers.

"Well, sire," the gnome spoke up. "We have to find him."

"Do you really think, Moth," he glowered at the little man, "that I need a dimwitted advisor to tell me that? Of course we need to find him."

Moth sulked back into the corner and avoided the annoyed stare coming from the red eyes of the sorcerer. His stare alone felt as though it would burn the wart right off the tip of the gnome's nose. Sarpene pivoted and headed straight for the door.

"Get my staff."

"Y-yes, sire, whatever you wish."

Moth scurried into another room and returned, clumsily following the black robes flowing from his master's shoulders down a set of winding stairs. When they reached the bottom, Sarpene mumbled a few words, pointed at the locked door, and pulled his hand back, opening his fingers and the lock at the same time.

"Wonderful," he said as he entered the hallway to see an eight-foot troll leaning against the wall, sleeping. Grabbing the staff, Sarpene hammered the sleeping troll.

"WAKE UP!"

"Mas-Master," the monster moaned with a start, rubbing his bony head. "Me not sleep. Me only rest eyes."

Sarpene reached up and pulled the troll down to eye level.

"Shut up and watch the door, and if your eyes need another rest, don't worry, I'll make sure they're closed for the next thousand years."

Slamming the troll back into place, Sarpene continued past cell after cell, sending the occupants dashing into the farthest corner. Every few cells, Moth would rush to the bars and growl at the prisoner, bringing even more whimpers and cries, that was, until Sarpene left him with a rap on the forehead. When the pair reached the far wall, Sarpene pushed his robes aside and raised both hands. After a few more words, he raised the staff and tapped the highest stone. The wall rumbled and parted, opening into a dark room. With a flick, a torch hanging from the wall lit, revealing nothing but three more solid walls, a low ceiling, and stone patterned floor. Without a word, Sarpene and Moth entered. The opening closed with another rumble, leaving the two standing alone in a door-less room.

"Narsapi domencho, enimbi."

The floor now growled and opened, exposing bars and two separated rooms. The occupants cowered away from the foreign light.

"Ah, brother, it's been awhile. How ever are you doing?" Sarpene crouched and rapped the bars on top of the cell as if he were knocking.

"What do you want, Sarpene?" weakly came from one of the rooms.

"Only to visit with you and your beautiful queen. And how are you doing, Queen Shanipa?"

No answer came forth.

"Well, that's not very nice. I've told you time and time again. I'll release you if you agree to be my queen."

"I'd rather kiss the wart on a toad's rear end," she answered coldly. "But I see you brought one of those with you too."

Moth kicked at the barred roof as Sarpene chuckled.

"Beautiful and clever," Sarpene said. "You do the elfish people proudly."

"Cut with the niceties," Fintabi interrupted, struggling to stand up. "What do you want?" Supporting himself against the wall with one hand, Fintabi's frail, bent body straightened as much as possible and through a sickly, sunken face, he glared at the sorcerer with proud eyes that hadn't weakened in eleven years.

"Brother," Sarpene said as he looked at Fintabi's frail body. "You don't look so well. Are you sure you're eating the right diet and getting plenty of exercise?"

"What do you want!?"

Sarpene smirked.

"Only to let you know that you don't have to be locked away for very much longer."

"What do you mean?" Fintabi hissed.

"A young warrior has finally shown his cowardly face again, and when he is destroyed, you will be as well."

"You serpent!" Fintabi cried, temporarily regaining the strength the jump up and grab the bars. "If you touch him, it'll be the last thing you do."

"No," Sarpene replied nonchalantly as his shadow hid the face of the angry king. With a flick, he sent sparks into Fintabi's hands and knocked him to the floor. "I think that after I slay your son, I'll do the same to your queen. Only I will let you watch that, knowing for eternity that you could do nothing to stop me."

With a wave of his hand, the floor closed again to the sound of both prisoners screaming. Turning to Moth, he gave his orders.

"Call upon everyone in the kingdom. Triple the scouts, wake up the giants, and spread the vultures. I want that brat found and brought to me before the moon is new."

Moth nodded and marched importantly through the opened wall.

"Soon," Sarpene snarled out loud, clenching his fist and bringing absolute darkness around him at the same time.

9

Wolf Fight

Creeping through the woods without a tremor from low-hanging branches or the brush surrounding him, Dantin moved soundlessly. With careful, narrowed eyes, he strained every sense as he tried to turn from prey to hunter.

—SNAP.

Reaching down, Dantin almost sighed with relief as he found and drew his sword, crouching even lower. Falling to one knee, he turned as a growl erupted from behind and brought a lunging beast with bared, yellow teeth hungry for blood. Thrusting his sword, Dantin bared his own teeth, stopped the wolf mid-lunge and dropped him with a dull thud against the ground.

Without a glance at his victim, Dantin regained his feet and brought his sword up again. Within a blink, another flash of fur and teeth rushed onto his left. Swinging his sword like a bat, he slammed the wolf to the ground and spun back just in time to crush another flash coming from the right.

"BRING IT!" he cried, regaining his stance and his surroundings.

Sensing another strike, he quickly hit the ground, rolled backwards, and caught a fourth pouncing wolf from underneath as if he'd known the attack before the wolf did. Rolling away, he once again was on his feet and stole a glance and smirk at the fallen wolves.

Distracted, Dantin missed the next strike and his back exploded in pain as two claws dug in and hot breath brought gnarled teeth chomping for his throat. Instinctively throwing himself down, Dantin bucked the wolf off with a strong spring from his legs and faced the beast. Grimacing against his wounds, Dantin stared into the cold eyes and lost his head to fury and pain. His own bloodshot eyes narrowed and grew cold. From behind his snarled lip, Dantin released a cry of fury and hate as he sprang. But his lost smirk reappeared on the wolf's face as Dantin's sword fell limp and landed harmlessly at the wolf's side. His horror-filled eyes raised just in time to find two more wolves springing on him from either side, ripping and tearing as his world went black.

"NO, NO, NO, NO, NO!!!!" an exasperated scream boomed in. Tenii appeared with arms raised to the sky. Instantly the woods and wolves disappeared and Dantin lay alone, facedown in a grassy meadow. Slamming his fists into the ground, he pushed himself to his feet and rubbed his sore shoulder. The wounds disappeared with the scene, but the sting was still there.

"MAN!" Dantin kicked at the grass, turned away from Tenii, and stared at the sky, hands on hips and chest heaving with an angry sigh.

"What happened?"

"I don't know," Dantin spat through gritted teeth. "I felt him on my back, and then I saw the look in his eyes, my brain exploded and I couldn't think anymore. ARRRGH, *every* time!"

Dantin threw his hands into the air and paced back and forth, keeping his eyes from meeting Tenii's.

"Relax, it will come, with time," Tenii comforted.

"Yeah, how much time do I need?"

"We've only been training for a few weeks."

"Yeah, but every day it happens the same way. I kill a few, then lose my head and get taken by the rest. It's like I'm not strong enough."

"You've got the strength to defeat them all," Tenii comforted as he stepped forward and put his hand on Dantin's shoulder. "It's not strength of body you should be worried about, you already have that. Strength in the mind will allow you to defeat anyone. It WILL come!

You must be patient and keep working."

Dantin pushed Tenii's hand from his shoulder and walked away, picking up the again razor sharp blade. He found a place in between a clump of trees and slumped to the ground with his head in his hands.

As he thought the whole simulation through, he realized that he was not actually mad at his performance. He'd done much better against these wolves than he'd ever done and Tenii told him that he'd grown much faster than even he'd hoped, but impatience was getting the better of him. Just yesterday a group of squirrels showed up with a report of wolves patrolling close to the edge of the Badlands. He pleaded with Tenii to allow him to go test his training in a real-life situation, but Tenii said he was not ready, and today's trial had proven him right. But Dantin could not help it; he *so* wanted to be ready. He had yet to have a night without nightmares of defeat. But recently, different dreams had come too. He was starting to dream of his parents and what it would be like to hug his mother and feel her loving arms around him. Running his hands through his hair he groaned and slammed them into the ground on either side of himself.

"Dantin," Tenii said as Dantin emerged an hour later, shoulders slumped as he slowly trudged back to the waiting dwarf. "You are being too hard on yourself. Just three weeks ago you were a scared little boy, not even wanting to go into the woods alone. Now look at you. You're turning into an excellent swordsman, your attention to your surroundings is astounding, and your instincts are growing with every breath you take."

"I know, I know," Dantin sighed, again averting Tenii's eyes. "But the only thing I think about is my family and them being tortured or something."

"And I too. I loved your father as if he were my brother. But our anxiousness cannot put our careful planning in danger. The enemy is too great, brute strength is useless. But a strong, calculating mind can overcome."

"Alright," Dantin said with a loud sigh of gaining confidence. "Let's try it again."

"No," Tenii smiled. "I realized while you were gone that we've been pushing it too hard. The stress is getting to both of us. I sent for Petra, and we are going to relax for a while."

Dantin's eyes brightened and finally rose to meet Tenii's. He had not seen his new friend for two weeks now. Tenii sent him away because he kept getting in the way. He was a bit over anxious, and greatly tested Tenii's patience, though his antics and Tenii's exasperated responses always brought a smile to Dantin's face. They were like Moe and Curly, leaving Dantin wondering if *he* were Larry.

Petra arrived that evening with more news from the Badlands.

"They're capturing every animal they can find and torturing them for information. The vultures are even traveling out of the Badlands. It's only a matter of time before they find us."

Tenii sighed and rubbed his beard, a gesture Dantin commonly saw when the dwarf thought.

"Then let's go after them," Dantin jumped in.

"Yeah, let's do it," Petra agreed.

"NO! It's out of the question."

"But—"

"NO!"

"Tenii," Dantin pleaded calmly. "How many creatures is Sarpene going to kill while we wait for *me* to be ready? You heard Petra say they were grabbing everyone they found. I can't wait much longer; they're being killed because of me. And sooner or later, one of them is going to give us away."

Without response, Tenii turned and began to walk away. When Petra called to him, he simply raised his hand to quiet him and continued to walk. Dantin and Petra looked at each other for an explanation, but neither seemed to know what to think.

When Tenii returned an hour later, Dantin was reenacting the simulation from earlier that day for Petra.

"I almost had it, then all of the sudden, blam. I blew it again."

"Wow, did you really get to—"

"Alright guys," Tenii said, interrupting the story. "If we're going to do this, there is much to do."

Dantin's eyes widened and he looked toward Petra with a great smile.

"Alright!" Dantin cheered, but then hesitated. "Wait. You said *we*, does that mean that you are going with me?"

"That we will again discuss later, right now we need to get you some *real* help."

"I'll help!" Petra jumped in.

"I'm sure you will, but I was thinking about warriors, dwarfish and elfin warriors, not fawns."

Petra gave him a reproachful look.

"Really?" Dantin asked, looking confused. "But I thought you said they were all killed when Sarpene took over?"

"Many were, but some fled to different areas and have been living in hiding. There is one dwarf in particular that we must find, Byron, one of the greatest dwarfish woodsmen there ever was. The last word of him was from deep within Kudosh forest, many, many miles to the southwest. If we find him, I'm sure he'll help. But we'll have to avoid the Badlands and Sarpene's scouts."

Dantin shivered at his memory of the Badlands, but still came with an argument, "Why go around the Badlands? Why don't we go straight through?"

"No," Tenii said forcefully. "You don't understand the dangers of the Badlands. They must be avoided at all cost for as long as possible."

"You must remember, Tenii," Dantin said defensively, "that I have already been in the Badlands, alone. I'm not too worried about what—"

"That's the problem," Tenii jumped in. "You're not worried enough. The taste you got of the Badlands was but a hair on the head of the beast. There are dangers and evils there that even I can't comprehend."

"But if we can get there quicker, then we can save more lives."

"If we don't get there at all, we don't save any lives."

"What if we're too late? Petra said that there are already vultures outside the Badlands. What makes us any safer out here?"

To this, Tenii had no response. His hand went to his beard.

"Besides," Dantin jumped on the hesitation. "If we are moving away from the castle, don't you think the scouts will be less and less frequent? Everyone will be surrounding the castle, or looking for us outside the Badlands."

Tenii still had no response. Dantin and Petra could see the gears spinning rapidly in his head, so Dantin made the deciding comment, flirting with crossing the line of going too far.

"If you're afraid, give me directions, and I'll go myself."

"AFRAID! You would do better to be *more* afraid." With that, Tenii stormed away again, afraid of what he may say next.

Dantin felt bad for his accusation. He knew that Tenii was doing his best, and that he had given Dantin nothing but friendship and support from the first time they met. He gave his friend a few minutes to cool off and went looking for him. He found him walking alone in a field, cursing himself aloud.

"Tenii, I'm sorry. I had no right to say that."

"No, young Dantin, you were more right than you imagine." Tenii turned and even through just the moonlight, Dantin could see remains of tears lost in the dwarf's beard. The sight almost brought Dantin to his knees. To see this strong little man weep scared Dantin more than anything else had yet.

"No. I wasn't right; I was completely out of line. You've been great to me and have really taught me a lot about my family and fighting and—"

"Yes, but never have I intended to accompany you on your quest," Tenii said with lowered eyes and a pale face.

Dantin stared at him bewildered. To this, *he* was speechless. After minutes of silence, the simplest, yet perhaps the most important, question came to his mind.

"But why?"

Tenii sighed and his eyes lowered even more.

"Ever since I was a young boy, I have lived in the shadow of Sarpene, just as he lived in your father's shadow. Though my father discovered his dark side before we finished our training, I was still outshined by him in everything we did. He never forgot important spells. He never spilled dragon phlegm on his father's book of spells. He never accidentally turned his mother into an insect."

Dantin choked down a chuckle.

"To make matters worse, he taunted me every chance he got. He never let me forget how much better he was than me. Even if I knew a spell well, all he had to do was mention it and I was sure to fail. I am afraid of him, but I'm afraid of myself as well. I'm afraid that if I lead you into the Badlands, I will be leading you into certain death. I can't handle Sarpene, and I would get you killed as well."

"But what good would I be without you?"

"You can't count on me. If we meet Sarpene, I'll freeze, and we will have both failed and the kingdom will completely die."

"I don't believe that. *I* have faith in you."

"Thank you," Tenii responded, his eyes raising for a split second. "But I fear that will not be enough."

"It's enough for me. And what of this Byron guy, if we can find him, you said he'd help too."

"I sure hope so."

"So when do we leave?"

Tenii hesitated and looked up at the full moon.

"Tomorrow."

"Together?"

Tenii's eyes met Dantin's again and stuck as he sighed.

"If you're willing to travel with a misfit wizard/dwarf that'll probably get you killed, then yes, we'll go through the Badlands together."

Dantin beamed as if a weight was lifted from his shoulders.

"Do you think there is any way we can talk Petra out of coming with us?" he asked, though he already knew the answer.

"I think we'd have a better chance of asking Sarpene to surrender without a fight."

Dantin's smile stretched across his face and he put his arm around his friend. They walked together in the dark toward the waiting Petra. Tenii stopped and stroked his beard as he looked around the darkened meadow.

"Now where is that pesky house?"

10

The Journey Begins

Through many frantic preparations, the three readied themselves. Tenii packed as much food as he could come up with, Petra searched the meadows and the trees for herbs and other spices Tenii instructed him to find, and Dantin practiced with his sword one last time against imaginary creatures in the meadow. They would have looked quite humorous to anyone who happened by, running around like chickens with their heads cut off.

"So how are we going to get to Byron, anyway?" Dantin asked he entered the house and took off his sweat-soaked shirt.

"It won't be easy. Kudosh is outside the Badlands, but it is a great forest with many creatures of its own, both good and evil. I've already sent pigeons ahead of us with a message. Hopefully they will find Byron first and let him know we're coming."

"What if we can't find him?" Petra broke in, returning with a satchel full of leaves.

"That is something I would rather not think about," Tenii answered shaking his head. "Then, I fear, all could be lost."

"Has anyone ever said that you were a tad bit overdramatic?" Dantin said rolling his eyes toward Petra.

"Perhaps, but my father always taught me that it is better to imagine the dangers worse and be over prepared than to take them lightly and not be prepared enough."

"Well, Ms. Mullin always taught me that if I imagined the worst, she would always find something worse than I could ever think of to completely surprise me. That's actually been the theme of my life." Dantin said this with a big smile, even though he was only half joking.

"Well, I was always taught," Petra said importantly, "life was like a bag of chocolate-covered insects: you never know what you're going to get."

Tenii smiled and shook his head.

"Any way you look at it, we're *going* to be prepared."

They finished packing up bags for each of them, and Tenii looked around the house to see if he was forgetting anything.

"One more thing," he sighed.

He left the room and returned with the decorated sword Dantin saw in the glass case his first day in Pangadesh.

"I can't leave without this."

Dantin looked confused.

"I thought you said you can't control that sword."

"Well," Tenii said with a sly smile. "It's always worth another try."

"What does it do, anyway?" Petra asked.

"I'll explain while we walk."

With that, all three tied up their bags and hoisted them upon their shoulders. Dantin took one more look at the Gladius Aspectus before sheathing it and heading out the door into another unfamiliar meadow.

"I've placed us as close to the Badlands as is safe," Tenii explained. "We should have a straight shot through to the Kudosh forest and we won't have to go much farther than the edge of the Badlands. If we travel swiftly, and no problems arise, we should make it through in about four days."

"Four days in there," Dantin said wide-eyed.

"It's the only way. Besides, you're the one who wanted to take the shorter route."

"I know, I know. Is it too late to change my mind," he said, again only half joking.

"I'm afraid not."

Without another word, the threesome took off toward the dark woods. As promised, Tenii explained his special sword.

"It is another one of my father's creations. Only wizards and sorcerers with great knowledge of spells can use it properly. It has the special power of reversing spells put upon you. If you are familiar with the spell being placed upon you, the sword acts as a shield and then reflects the spell back upon its originator. But problems arise when a user does not know that particular spell. In that case, the sword is useless. You even have to know a specific spell for the sword to be useful in a battle; otherwise it would be like a wooden stick."

Dantin and Petra listened intently to the story of the sword. Dantin kept quiet his fears that Tenii would not be able to remember the spells well enough and that Sarpene would kill him with a snap of his fingers. Pushing this thought from his mind, Dantin changed the subject to Byron.

"Why has Byron been hiding for so long? If he's a great warrior, why has he not yet fought back?

"Even great warriors have to bide their time," Tenii answered. "Just as I wish we could spend more time and effort in your training, biding our time as well. But sometimes, action is the only answer."

"Is one warrior going to be enough against Sarpene and the rest of his creatures?"

Tenii scratched his beard.

"I have heard rumors that Byron has started up small resistance groups from dwarves and other creatures that may be willing to help."

Petra perked up and joined the conversation.

"He has an army?"

"No, I don't think you can call his small band an army. But if there is any truth to the rumors, they could be very helpful to us."

The three spent the rest of the morning and much of the afternoon with similar conversations about who might help, how they were going to attack, and other various topics that showed themselves. But as the sun slowly began to fall from the sky, Dantin looked ahead and saw that the dark line of trees that had been very distant now looked large and scary. He glanced behind to see the peach sun, falling through pink clouds and making the sky glow a weird purple color. The scene was so calm and perfect, he couldn't believe that when he turned again, he would be facing a gray, ugly evil. They seemed like two different worlds, one beautiful, colorful and full of friendship and love, and the other dreary and hateful.

They continued in silence for some time. Each was too busy trying to talk the fear from themselves. When they finally reached the edge of the woods, Tenii looked around, scratched his beard, and made a suggestion.

"Perhaps we should camp here for the night. We still have a couple hours of daylight, but once we're in the Badlands, there won't be much difference between daytime and nighttime."

"Fine with me," Dantin agreed.

Petra jumped on the suggestion as well.

"The more we can delay going in there, the better. Besides, if I don't stop and eat now, my stomach is going to collapse."

"Fine then," Tenii said, very much relieved. "Let's find a safe place and hold up."

"Great," Petra said. "I'll gather some firewood."

"No," Dantin and Tenii said in unison.

"Why not, it's going to be dark soon. How are we going to see?"

"The less we can see," Tenii explained, "the less likely dangers will be able to see us. A fire is an invitation for every creature around to visit us, good and evil."

Dantin and Petra did, however, gather branches and leaves, and with the help of a spell from Tenii, they had a camouflaged shelter to sleep in. When all was prepared, the three sat down and relaxed for the first time. Dantin pulled out food for the three of them as Tenii looked out the opening and saw the sun was nearly gone now, hiding behind some distant mountains.

"I guess all we can do now is eat and try to rest. We can leave at first light."

"Tenii," Petra began as he lay back. "What kind of creatures are we going to run into in there?"

"Just before we go to sleep, Petra, I'm sure we can find a more cheerful conversation."

"No," Dantin said. "I'd like to know as well. I want to know what to expect before I'm face to face with a monster."

"Well," Tenii sighed, "you've already met some wolves, and you've heard stories of vultures, but there are far worse creatures within that forest. Owls use their keen eyesight to patrol the night, and rats act as snitches to any intruders. There are trolls, some only my size, but others have grown half as tall as a tree. But trolls are easy to avoid. They bring with them the most horrible smell imaginable, giving you at least a half mile's warning. Though there are not many, Sarpene has control over some dwarves and elves. Nobody knows if they turned to Sarpene's side by choice, or whether they are controlled by a spell, but they can be very dangerous because they know everything about the woods, hiding places, escape routes, and other useful things. And, there are also the giants."

With every description, the eyes of Dantin and Petra grew three sizes. They both began to regret wanting to know what lay beyond the tree line.

"But the most dangerous of all evils within the forest are the spells put on ordinary objects. There is a stream somewhere that is meant to turn friends against each other. It is said that anyone who drinks from it will attack even his closest friend. I have also heard of enchanted trees. They are placed here and there around the forest. They look no different than regular ones, but if you get too close, their branches will close upon you and crush you."

Dantin was speechless as he looked at Tenii's serious face. He'd heard a lot of scary stories before, like the one about the man with a hook instead of a hand, searching through the woods for someone else's hand to steal, and Tommy's favorite story about cannibals coming to eat the first person who falls asleep. But this story was by far the worst ever because he knew that any of the creatures in Tenii's story could be lurking within a few feet of them right now.

"But, these are things that we do not need to worry about right now," Tenii finally said, seeing the looks of horror in his companions' eyes. "Right now, we need to get some sleep and make sure we are rested. It may be a long time before we can sleep again, so we need to get as much of it as possible."

Dantin rolled his eyes.

"Yeah, like I'm sleeping."

"Me either," Petra followed.

"Well, I can take care of that," Tenii said. With a quiet word and a snap of his fingers, their heads fell, and they were out. He lowered his head as well, but then jumped up to make sure his friends were still breathing.

"Whew," he said, wiping his forehead. "I finally got that one right."

11

Bad Blood

Even with the help sleeping, Dantin's night was still filled with nightmares about trolls and giants. The worst one left him running alone through the woods without a weapon, being chased by a hundred-foot monster. It ended abruptly when he was grabbed and gobbled up. He woke up and shook his head in disgust. He looked out of the shelter and saw that it was still dark. But it was a strange darkness, different than it had been when they fell asleep. It had an eerie feeling, like a heavy weight on his shoulders, and the air seemed thick and dirty as he breathed.

"Tenii, wake up,"

Tenii mumbled a few words and his eyes struggled to open.

"What is it?" he groaned.

"Look outside."

Tenii wiped the sleep from his eyes and sat up with another groan, but as soon as he looked outside the shelter, his eyes popped wide open and he jumped to his feet.

"We have to go, NOW! Wake Petra up."

"But, why—"

"There's no time for questions, get Petra and let's go."

Tenii left the shelter and looked around outside. Dantin struggled to wake the sleeping deer.

"Come on, Petra, wake up, let's go," he repeated over and over. Finally the deer stirred and groggily lifted his head.

"What do you want?" he asked in an annoyed grumble.

"There's danger, we have to go."

Without another word, Petra's eyes burst open and he jumped up. The two fled the shelter to find Tenii wandering about, looking in all directions. Dantin looked around and recognized the field from the previous day, but it was changed somehow. The dreariness left him feeling very uncomfortable.

"What's going on Tenii, why is it still so dark?"

"We're in the Badlands."

"WHAT?" Dantin and Petra yelled together. "How did that happen?"

"I'll explain later. Plug your noses."

Tenii snapped his fingers, spoke some quiet words, and the three felt a strong breeze. Dantin gagged at the horrible stench he remembered from weeks ago.

"Another cow pasture, huh."

Ignoring the comment, Tenii picked up his pack, scanned the area one more time, decided on a direction, and took off.

"Grab your packs, let's go."

Petra and Dantin grabbed everything they could and followed Tenii into the woods. Strangely, they were too rushed and confused to be scared.

They traveled slowly and carefully for what seemed like an eternity before Dantin could not take it anymore.

"Tenii," he said in a loud whisper. "Hold on. What happened back there?"

"Well," he said, stopping and scanning the surroundings again. "Sarpene must have extended the Badlands somehow. I didn't think it was possible, but he did it before I had a chance to protect us."

"How far does it reach now?"

"I don't know, but it's a good thing we left yesterday. Who knows what kind of creatures are hanging out where we were. We were lucky not to be discovered during the night."

Dantin's heart began to race. Were they being watched now? Was there a wolf behind one of these trees waiting to pounce on them?

Without another thought, he drew his sword and kept it in a ready position as the three moved on. They traveled for another few hours before they finally stopped to rest.

"We need to eat," Tenii said after making sure the spot they stopped at was safe.

Dantin's empty stomach growled its agreement at the mention of food. He took off his pack and searched through it for their food. His heart sank and he looked up at his companions with wide eyes. Without a word, he frantically searched again. Finally, he turned the pack upside down and dumped all the contents onto the ground.

"It-it's not here," he said.

"What's not here?" Petra asked, getting a little scared himself.

"The food, it's not here?"

"Well, where is it?" Petra's voice was beginning to rise.

"I-I don't know. I swear I packed it before we left the camp."

"Look again," Tenii said calmly.

"I did! It's not here!"

"Calm down, calm down. It's going to be alright."

"How is it going to be alright, Tenii? Without food, how are we going to survive four or five days in this place?"

"And you said that I was over dramatic," Tenii said with a smile. "There are ways we can survive, but I'm not sure you're going to like them."

Dantin's stomach did a somersault.

"Bugs?"

"That's right. I told you they were warriors' food?"

Dantin felt the color drain from his face and his mouth got sticky. If he would have had anything in his stomach, he would have lost it right there at the mere thought.

"I guess it's not that bad, Dantin," Petra comforted. "We've been eating insects for thousands of years."

Dantin nearly lost it again. He shook the thought from his head and pleaded with Tenii.

"Can't you just make more of that bark stuff? At least that way I won't have to taste the bugs."

"I wish I could, but it's too dangerous. Remember when I told you that Sarpene could detect me using spells in the Badlands? If he were anywhere near, it'd be the end of it. It was a big enough risk just to mask our scents."

As Tenii explained, Petra began to flip rocks over and found plump beetle.

"See, Dantin," he said through his teeth. "It isn't that bad." He sucked it in and chewed it up.

That was more than Dantin could handle. He fell to his knees and scrambled to a tree while his stomach screamed to release the nothing it contained. Dantin coughed and choked horribly for a few minutes before his stomach gave up and relaxed. He rolled over with closed eyes and ran his hand through his matted hair.

Tenii looked comfortingly upon him.

"Relax for a few minutes. We're going to go—well, just rest, we'll be right back."

Tenii and Petra searched around for more insects. They each ate a few they found, and stored away a few more. When they returned, Dantin was standing, upset with himself for what happened.

"I'm sorry about that, guys, I don't know what came over me."

"Don't worry about it, young Dantin. If we were back where you came from, and I had to watch someone eat a hamburger, I'd be doing the same thing." Tenii shivered and shook the thought from his head.

Dantin smiled.

"So what are we going to do? I can't eat that stuff."

"We're going to keep going. When you get to the point where it is either eat and survive or not eat and starve, your body will give in and accept the food."

"What if it doesn't?"

"Then your strong will is going to have to force it to."

"Wonderful."

Dantin struggled as they continued to keep his mind off of his empty stomach. He went over his battle plan if they were discovered at least a hundred times, he thought about the first conversation he was going to have with his parents, and he even amused himself thinking about how if Ms. Mullin were with them, she'd have starved hours ago, or maybe she'd have tried to eat Petra. Smiling and shaking his head, he continued in the path Tenii led. The further they got, the darker and drearier it seemed to get.

"How much further until we stop?" he whispered ahead.

Tenii looked up and around at the surroundings.

"In a couple more hours, it'll be too dark to travel. We'll have to keep going until then."

Dantin didn't respond, but Petra groaned behind them. Dantin's legs began to wobble, but he forced himself to go on.

The rest of the day went by in a haze. Dantin was no longer able to concentrate on a single thought without his mind going back to food. His legs simply moved automatically, bringing his body with them as his mind wandered randomly from thought to thought. When they finally stopped, he sat down and fell asleep before Tenii had even found them a shelter.

Tenii looked around and found a spot hidden away under a couple of boulders.

"We should be safe there," he said to Petra. "Here, help me with Dantin."

The two of them helped carry the sleeping boy to the shelter. When they had him safely put away, Petra went to search for food. He returned a few minutes later and found Tenii sitting over Dantin, stroking the boy's hair.

"Will he eat?" Petra asked.

"I sure hope so," he answered, sighing and shaking his head.

Petra and Tenii stayed up and talked for a few minutes until they both fell asleep where they sat.

Dantin's sleep was again plagued by horrible dreams, but these ones were all centered on food and water. In one, he found himself burning up in what had to be at least 120 degrees. He was surrounded by nothing but sand, and the blazing sun burned into his soul. He drug himself up and down sand dune after sand dune, struggling to stay on his feet. At one point, he spotted an oasis, but when he tried to drink, he got nothing but a mouthful of sand. He awoke in the middle of the night to his stomach feeling like he'd been shot with an arrow. He rolled over and over, holding the ache and moaning. Finally, he sat up, knowing what he had to do.

Straining his eyes against the almost pitch black, he stumbled out of the shelter and found a dead tree limb lying on the ground. Willing himself to continue, he rolled it over and right there was an enormous beetle. Without even thinking about it, he scooped it up and swallowed it whole, washing it down like an aspirin with his canteen.

Desperately trying not to think about what he had just done, his mind betrayed him and gave him an image of the beetle crawling around in his empty stomach.

That was it. Up it came with an awful force as Dantin fell to his knees.

"Come on, you wimp," he yelled angrily to himself, wiping his mouth. "You can do this."

He decided that he must kill the insect before he ate it, but chewing it up was out of the question. He found another beetle and mashed it in his fingers. Again without thinking he popped it and washed it down with twice as much water. He went through a few agonizing minutes of gagging and almost throwing up before his stomach finally relented and accepted the food. Regaining his courage, Dantin repeated the process with five more bugs. Each time his stomach tried to send them back up, but he concentrated hard on keeping them down. After he choked down the sixth one, his stomach began to swell. It was mostly water, but that was good enough for now. He returned to the shelter and found Tenii sitting up waiting for him.

"I'm proud of you, Dantin. You do have a very strong will."

"No big deal," Dantin brushed off the compliment. "Just don't make me eat any snails. That escargot stuff makes me sick."

Tenii smiled and lay back down. Dantin did the same and fell into a sleep not completely free from nightmares, but much more peaceful than it had been all night.

What seemed like no more that five minutes later, Tenii shook him awake.

"Dantin, we must go."

Dantin rolled over and groaned. His stomach felt empty again, but the ache from the previous day had subsided. He pushed himself to his feet and saw Petra wandering about searching for more bugs. They ate a quick breakfast and Dantin forced himself to imagine he was eating runny eggs and blueberry pancakes. It helped and his stomach reluctantly gave in.

"Let's get a move on," Tenii said. "We've got a long way to travel today."

As they traveled, Dantin's mind wandered around everything that was happening and smiled at how uneventful their journey had been so far. Shaking his head, he chased the thought from his head. He knew that when he thought such things, fate had a way of proving him wrong.

"Alright," Tenii stopped in a small clearing and turned. "Let's rest for a few minutes."

"Phew," Dantin replied, wiping his sweaty forehead. "I thought we were never going to stop."

"Me either," Petra followed.

"You guys stay here for a few minutes; I'm going to go check things out."

Petra and Dantin sat down and rested while Tenii disappeared behind a bush. After a few minutes, Dantin felt a tiny prick on the back of his neck. Slapping it, he pulled his hand around and found a smashed mosquito. Shrugging his shoulders, he popped it in his mouth, smiling to himself that he didn't even have to chase it with water this time. Closing his eyes, he rested until Tenii returned and got them moving again.

"Alright, guys, that's enough. Let's go."

Both Petra and Dantin sighed as they stood up and followed.

"How much further do we have to go?" Dantin asked as they started to walk.

"We've made pretty good time so far," Tenii replied. "My guess is that we have another two and a half days before we reach the edge of Kudosh forest. Hopefully, the magic of the forest has not allowed the Badlands to stretch that far."

As they continued, Dantin's head began to feel light. He looked around and the forest seemed to spin around him. Shaking his head and forcefully blinking his eyes, he tried to concentrate on Tenii's back.

"Kill the dwarf, he's leading you into a trap!"

The voice boomed from all around him, like he was surrounded by hidden speakers.

"Who said that?" Dantin yelled, clumsily drawing his sword and taking an awkward stance.

"Kill them both, they are going to kill you!"

"Who are you?"

"Kill them NOW!"

"NOOOOO!" Dantin dropped his sword, fell to his knees and curled over covering his ears. Sweat poured down his forehead. Rolling into a fetal position, he began to lose consciousness.

"DANTIN! What's going on?" Tenii and Petra ran to him as fast as they could. Tenii reached out and put a hand on his shoulder. Dantin's body thrashed in horrible seizures and he swatted Tenii's hand away. Suddenly he was on his feet again. Pushing through his confused friends, he found his sword and stumbled away.

"Tenii has been lying to you all along. He killed your parents years ago. Your quest is only to torture you for surviving. Kill him and return to Sarpene. He's your only family left."

"NO, NO, NO, NO, NO!" Dantin screamed trying to focus his eyes and steadying himself against a small tree. "Go away, stop talking to me!"

"I'll stop when they are dead!"

Dantin swung his sword with all his might, slicing through the small tree.

"That's it, now get the dwarf and fawn!"

Dantin swung wildly through the air as the voice laughed. He stopped and his head hung low as his chest heaved up and down. He pushed his hair from his face and raised his head, revealing an ear-to-ear grin. His eyes glossed over and he took an attack stance with his sword raised, again steadying himself with his free hand.

"Dantin?" Tenii mumbled quietly as he and Petra reached him. "What's going on?"

"You killed my parents!" he screamed, stepping toward them and stumbling again.

"Dantin, no—"

"DON'T LIE TO ME!" He swung his sword toward Tenii and Petra lunged at his back. Bringing the sword back, he caught the fawn in the side of the head with the hilt and sent him sprawling to the ground.

"That's it, Dantin. Kill him."

Barely glancing at the motionless fawn at his feet, Dantin turned his attention back to Tenii. Blinking again, he tried to clear his eyes and staggered forward.

"Dantin," Tenii sputtered. "You're under a spell. Just stop and—"

From deep within his soul, an evil cry erupted from Dantin's mouth as he raised his sword and lunged, bringing the sword down with all his might.

"Dantin, NO—" Tenii cried. Just as the sword was brought down up on him, a flash from his fingers hit Dantin and both their worlds went black.

12

Spies

"Dantin, can you hear me?"

"Dantin, can you hear me?" It repeated again and again.

"Tenii, what's happening?" Petra choked.

"He's under a spell." Tenii sat with Dantin's head in his lap. His colorless face beaded sweat and his body went into small convulsions every few seconds.

Petra's eyes widened as he rubbed the lump on his head.

"Is he going to—?"

"I don't know. Get the herbs I had you gather."

"Yeah, right here." Petra shakily passed his pack over. Tenii reached for it too fast and a piercing pain shot through his side. He gingerly rubbed it. Searching through the packet, he found four specific leaves.

"I have to make a fire," he said, gently laying Dantin's head on the ground.

"What if someone sees it?"

"We can't worry about that right now."

Tenii touched Dantin's burning head and wiped the sweat away with his shirtsleeve.

"He's feverish. If I don't stop it now, he's going to die."

Petra nearly fainted. Tenii mashed the leaves together in a small bowl and added a touch of water. He built a tiny fire and brought the mixture to a boil, adding spices to it from a bottle that looked like a saltshaker. After letting it cool for a few minutes, he funneled it into Dantin's mouth.

"Is that going to work?"

"If there is one thing that I do know," Tenii said, again wiping Dantin's head, "it's potions. These leaves are specially grown and if mixed with the right materials, can reduce a fever. The spell is another story, however. I need to know how it came about to break it."

Tenii searched Dantin's entire body for scrapes, scratches, or anything that might give him a clue as to how he was infected. He finally examined Dantin's neck and found a tiny bump.

"Mosquito," he said to himself.

"What?"

"Dantin was bitten by a mosquito. But I don't understand, a bite could not have transferred enough blood for this kind of a spell."

Tenii rubbed his beard.

"He must have eaten it."

"Eaten a mosquito?" Petra was taken aback. "But why? Everyone knows they're tainted."

"He must have, it's the only way."

"Can you break it?"

"It'll take some time, but I think so."

Petra looked on, pacing back and forth as Tenii searched his brain for the right spell.

"Help me, Father," he said aloud. "I've only got one shot at this."

Then suddenly, as if Pairton had been listening, a soft breeze came through and Tenii's eyes brightened.

"I have it!" he yelled.

Petra nearly jumped on top of him to hug him.

Tenii stood up, spread his arms apart, and began to chant. A quick flash came from his fingers and landed on Dantin. The flash only lasted a split second, but Tenii looked around to make sure no one was around to see it.

"Did it work?" Petra blurted, unable to hold back.

"We'll have to wait and see."

Tenii made a quick camp and sat for the rest of the night with Dantin's head in his lap. His fever had broken, but he still thrashed about every few minutes and would not wake up. Petra sat there and looked at his sick friend.

"Anything yet?" he would ask from time to time.

"Nothing." Tenii would repeat, without even the slightest hint of annoyance. He too was asking himself that same question over and over. After much waiting, Petra's eyes grew too heavy and the fawn fell asleep where he sat. Tenii continued to stroke Dantin's matted red hair and look upon him as a mother would look upon her sick child. The night wore on and it was Tenii's turn to give in to heavy eyelids.

Hours later, Tenii was awakened by a rustling outside the shelter. He gently moved Dantin's head from his lap and tried to get up, but found his legs paralyzed. He slapped them a few times to wake them up and felt tiny pinpricks throughout his body.

"Petra," he called in a severe whisper. "Petra, wake up!" He picked up a stick and threw it at the fawn.

Startled awake, Petra jumped to his feet.

"What? Who? Why?" The confused fawn looked all around.

"SHHHHHH! There's something outside."

But it was too late. They both heard the rustle again as the creature scurried away.

"Go see what it is."

"Are you crazy?" Petra said in horror. "I'm not going out there alone."

"Petra, please," Tenii pleaded. "If that was one of Sarpene's spies, we'll be surrounded by wolves by tomorrow afternoon, if not sooner."

"Fine." Petra poked his head out of the shelter, took a quick look, and pulled it back in. "Nothing."

"You have to go outside." By this time, Tenii's legs were on fire with thousands of pinpricks on every inch.

Petra shook his head and left the shelter. He looked all around, but couldn't hear or see anything.

"Anything?" Petra nearly jumped out of his skin at the voice. He spun and found Tenii dragging a stubborn leg behind him.

"Jeez, are you trying to scare me to death? No, there's nothing. Maybe you were just hearing things."

"You heard it too, Petra."

"Yeah, well, maybe I was hearing things."

All of a sudden they heard a groan from the shelter. They both sprinted back to find Dantin struggling to push himself up to a sitting position.

"Dantin!" they cried in unison. They both jumped him and hugged him tightly.

"Hey, hey, hey, careful?" Dantin winced as it felt like lumberjacks were chopping wood in his skull. "What's going on?"

"Thank goodness you're alive," Tenii sobbed.

"I thought you were dead," Petra followed.

"I feel like I am dead. What happened?" he repeated, wincing each time he moved.

"You were under a spell."

"A SPELL! What kind of spell?"

"You were infected with tainted blood. I think it was from a mosquito."

"Mosquito? But when—? Oh man," he said, falling back down and covering his face with his hands. "I was stung on the neck and I ate it."

"That is what I thought," Tenii said.

"And Tenii saved you," Petra chimed in.

Dantin could see glowing cheeks through the dwarf's beard.

Dantin closed his eyes and sighed, trying not to move.

"Yeah, even after you attacked us."

"PETRA," Tenii scolded.

"Attacked you?" Dantin forgot the pain and shot straight up. "What are you talking about?"

Tenii shot the embarrassed deer a disapproving look and told Dantin the story.

"You turned on Petra and me with your sword. But luckily, the spell filled you with hate, so all you left me with was this."

Tenii lifted his shirt and revealed a purplish yellow bruise reaching from the dwarf's waist to his shoulders.

"Who would have thought rubber could leave such a mark," Tenii said.

"And you knocked me out," Petra followed, lowering his head for Dantin to fell the large lump.

"Guys, I'm sooo sorry. I-I didn't mean to—"

"I know, I know. Think nothing of it, my friend. That is what I'm here for. But that is enough recapping. We have to get out of here. Can you walk?"

"I-I think so," Dantin said through gritted teeth as he struggled to stand up. "Why am I so sore?"

"The spell attacked your brain and your muscles. They've been clenched all night. Hurry, I'm afraid we may have been discovered."

Without a second's hesitation, Dantin completely forgot all of his soreness and was out of the shelter ready to go.

"Which way?"

"I'm not sure," Tenii responded.

He stood there stroking his beard for a few seconds before he came to a decision.

"That way, let's go."

Without even looking to see if Dantin and Petra were following, Tenii took off in the direction he pointed. Dantin took one last stretch to get the kinks out and looked toward Petra.

"Come on, buddy. I promise not to try to kill you again."

"Yeah, I hope not," Petra responded with a smile.

As they traveled, Dantin's head began to slowly clear, but he could still feel the effects of the spell. Now and then he would get woozy and have to be supported by Petra. Every once in a while he would spot something moving out of the corner of his eye, but it would disappear before he could look at it fully.

"There," he called on one of these occasions.

"Where?" Petra responded, freezing with fear.

"I don't know, but it was there, in between those trees." Dantin squatted and squinted his eyes, but nothing was there.

"Go ahead and get Tenii," he whispered, drawing his sword. Petra jumped up and ran ahead, finding Tenii squatted next to a tree looking very worried.

"Tenii, Dantin thought he saw something again. Back here."

"Shhh, quiet. I felt something too." The two made their way back to Dantin. He was now inching his way around close to the ground, looking around intently.

"What did you see?" Tenii whispered.

"I'm not sure. That was the third or fourth time, but I'm still not sure. I'm still feeling very weird. The spell might still be messing with my head."

"Perhaps," Tenii said, following Dantin's gaze. "But I felt something weird as well. I can't tell what it was. I just felt the presence of another being."

"What's going on, guys? I can't feel anything."

"Shhh, Petra. Just wait," Tenii said, not pulling his eyes off the spot in between the two trees Dantin pointed out.

"How far are we away from Kudosh?" Dantin asked. "Could it be Byron?"

"We're still a day's journey away. I doubt very much Byron would travel this far into the Badlands without a particular reason."

"What if the pigeons found him and told him we were coming?" Petra added.

"Again, I doubt it. I don't think Byron is that easy to find."

"So what do we do?"

"We keep moving. Evil or not, being discovered can only lead to more danger. Let's just hope there aren't any wolves in the area."

As they discussed what to do, a pair of unseen eyes circled above. As soon as the bird got enough information, it headed directly north, to the heart of the Badlands.

13

Moth

"Sire, we've got news," panted Moth, scampering past the guards and into the dark chambers.

"What now?" sighed the annoyed sorcerer. "This had better be good."

"Yes, sire, it is. One of the ravens spotted three travelers in the far southern Badlands, about ten miles north of the Kudosh forest."

"Were they identified?"

"Well—no, sire, he didn't get close enough to see who it was, but—"

"Moth, tell me something. What good are spies that can't tell me if intruders are simple stragglers who took a wrong turn, or THE ENEMY, COMING TO TAKE OVER MY KINGDOM!" Moth jumped as Sarpene's fist slammed the throne and a fire grew in the back of his empty eyes.

"Well, I-I—"

"And what good," Sarpene began, standing up and approaching the quivering gnome, "is a dimwitted advisor that cannot tell me either?"

The gnome trembled as he backed away from the angry sorcerer into the corner. Running out of room, he came up with the best explanation his little mind would allow.

"It-it must be Tenii and the boy. They-they're flanking us to throw us off."

"No," Sarpene said thoughtfully, turning and leaving the gnome cowering in the corner. "Not even Tenii is fool enough to attack me on his own. You said they are near Kudosh?"

"Y-yes, sire."

"Do we have any enemies that prove a threat in Kudosh?"

"Well, I-I don't exactly know."

"Moth, let's get something straight." Turning, Sarpene again approached the gnome with clenched fists, and the small fire in the back of his eyes had grown into an inferno of anger. "If you wish to keep your position, as well as your tongue, I had better never again hear you say '*I don't know.*'"

The gnome's knees gave out and now he lay heaped on the floor, as a shirt would be after being tossed. Sarpene picked him up with one hand and held him against the wall, his feet three feet from the ground.

"Now I'll ask you again. Are there any *legitimate* threats in the Kudosh forest?"

"I-I don't—" the gnome began, stopping himself just in time as he saw the fire in Sarpene's eyes grow and tell him that his master meant every word of his threat. "There have been reports in the past that a group of rebel dwarves occupies Kudosh, but they have done nothing but minor damages to the edge of the Badlands and a few wolves and vultures that strayed too far into the forest. But we've never been able to take them out because it was too far from the castle."

"Can we attack them now?"

"I don't—" Again the gnome closed his eyes and he concentrated on not losing his life. "Yes, we can."

"And who leads this hoard?" Sarpene turned and let the gnome splatter back onto the floor.

"I believe it is a dwarf named Byron, but I doubt he is more than a pathetic coward."

"Hmm, Byron," Sarpene responded, slithering back toward the throne. "I have heard of him, which makes him more of a threat than your simple mind would know."

"Yes, sire," Moth responded, standing up, but not emerging from the corner.

"Are there any wolves in the area of the intrusion?"

"Yes, there is a pack of five or six about ten miles away. They are returning from a patrol."

"Send them after the intruders. After they are wiped out, send them into Kudosh to destroy anyone else they find."

"But, master, would it be wise—"

"Are you questioning my order?" Sarpene turned for a third time and Moth's knees gave out again.

"N-no, sire, right away." Moth scurried out of the room like a dog with his tail tucked between his legs before Sarpene could get any closer. Flying down the stairs, he found a hyena standing in a torch-lit hallway.

"Send the raven that brought news of the intruders back and have him find the closest pack of wolves to take care of them. Then have them move into Kudosh and destroy whatever they find," he ordered the hyena.

The hyena nodded and took off as Moth leaned against the wall and sighed, but he was unaware how close he really was from being destroyed himself.

14

Byron of Kudosh

"How much further, Tenii, the blisters around my hooves are growing blisters themselves," Petra whined after the three had traveled in silence for hours.

"Not much further now. We should get to Kudosh in a few hours, but as I said before, if the Badlands have extended into the forest, our journey does not get any easier."

"Any chance you can give us some good news for a change," Dantin said. His head had finally completely cleared, but he still had the weird feeling they were being watched.

"Sorry, Dantin, I gotta tell it like it is," Tenii said with a smile.

"When I become king, bad news is going to be illegal. Everyone will have to be positive."

"Then you're going to have to banish Tenii, I think bad news is the only news he knows of."

All three chuckled at the much-needed break in the tension. Dantin even finally released his constant grip on the hilt of his sword and noticed how sore his hand had become. Trying to work out the cramps, he turned to Tenii with more talk of the kingdom.

"So are you to be my royal wizard, Tenii?"

"No, Dantin," Tenii sighed. "Once the kingdom is restored, I'm sure more wizards will come out of hiding with much more power than I."

"But don't I get to choose my own advisors?"

"Yes, but like I said, there are better choices than me."

"Here we go again with the negativity," Dantin laughed. "I may have to banish you after all. Why don't you just—"

A howl in the distance interrupted the cheerful conversation and nearly stopped the hearts of all three travelers.

"Wh-what was that?" Petra asked.

"Let's go, this way, now." Tenii ushered them past a few bushes and into a break in the trees where they could turn around. Dantin re-gripped his sword and crouched down as Tenii used Petra's back to climb a tree to get a better look.

"Where are they?" Dantin whispered.

"North, about five hundred yards."

"How many?"

"It looks like five, maybe six wolves."

Dantin choked down a lump in his throat and look with wide eyes as the fawn's knees began to quiver.

"Are you ready?" Tenii asked as he jumped down.

"You know I am," Dantin answered struggling to keep a hold of his emotions.

Tenii drew his own sword and looked into the boy's eyes, seeing the fear hidden behind the confidence.

"Petra, find a place to hide. If anything happens to us, carefully make your way toward Kudosh. Find Byron and let him know what happened. Dantin, you take the right. Anything that comes through those trees loses his head, got it?"

"I'm on it." Dantin twirled his sword around and crouched into a ready position. Tenii did the same on the left as they heard the growls and beat of many feet getting closer.

"Spread out, they're around here somewhere. You two go that way. You and you go that way. Kill anything with a pulse."

Dantin's heart slammed through his chest like bongos. He fingered the hilt in his sweaty palm and crouched even closer to the ground, behind a large bush. Just on the other side he could hear the raspy breaths of a wolf searching for his scent. He froze, fighting the thoughts in his head to run away.

No, he thought, forcing himself to hold his ground. *I'm not leaving them behind.*

As the sniffing rounded the bush, Dantin called upon every ounce of courage within him. Thinking of his mother, he smiled and called the plays in his head.

Not yet, not yet. A little closer, that's it. Almost—NOW!

Dantin sprung at the beast and with one clean swoop the wolf lay lifeless, unable to alert the others. He crouched back down and looked for the next attacker, finding him about fifteen yards in front of him. But the wolf discovered him at the same time. He let go of a nasty bark and came barreling toward him. Dantin turned his head and spotted another large bush and took off around it. The wolf leapt around the other side to meet him in the back, but found nothing. He howled again and searched for the scent. A second later, Dantin emerged behind the confused beast. Before he knew what hit him, the wolf lay lifelessly at Dantin's feet, just as his partner did only seconds before.

As he crept forward, Tenii wondered if he were just as scared as Dantin. While he looked around, every attack spell he ever learned swirled around in his head and jumbled together. Two wolves rounded either side of the large tree he was crouched behind. He stood and pushed himself as close to the tree as possible, wishing he could crawl inside and hide until it was all over. Then, all of a sudden he felt a small breeze on his face and he got an idea as if he felt Pairton speaking from above. Seeing a low-hanging branch directly above his head, he swung up and was on top of the branch before either of the wolves rounded the tree. Hearing a scuffle, both wolves rushed around and banged heads right where Tenii had been.

"Where'd he go, I just heard him?"

"I don't know. I thought—"

"Up here, guys."

Just as both wolves looked up, they were hit with a perfect freezing spell. Tenii laughed as he jumped down and finished the wolves with his sword before the stun wore off. But before he could congratulate himself too much, he heard a scream.

"Tenii, Dantin. HELP!"

Petra was backed against two large trees and two nasty wolves were slowly circling him, ready to pounce. Tenii immediately looked toward Dantin, but they were both too far away to get there in time.

"NOOOOO!" Dantin screamed as the first wolf sprung at the defenseless deer.

From the sky, an arrow flew in and stopped the wolf in mid-flight. Everyone's head, including the remaining wolf's, snapped to where the arrow had come from, but nothing could be seen in the shadows.

After a few confused seconds, two figures appeared on either side of the tree Petra was backed against.

"DOLO!" erupted from high above and Dantin looked up again to find a third figure swinging down. The cry made the hairs on the back of his neck stand straight up.

The wolf wildly glanced at the figures in front of him, then up to the figure swinging toward him, and took off, but it was too late. Letting go of the vine, the figure landed smoothly just in front of the wolf, stopping him in his tracks.

"Where do you think you're going?" he called.

The wolf growled and jumped at him, but he coolly pulled a battleaxe from behind his back and relieved the wolf of his head in mid-flight. He spat on the body and looked toward the two figures on either side of Petra.

"Search the area, make sure that was the last of them," he called. The other two nodded with a smile and took off without a word. They returned a few minutes later.

"All clear, Byron. If there were any more, they've run off," the first figure said. As they got closer, Dantin could see their long, scruffy beards and puckered noses.

"Byron, from Kudosh?" Tenii asked.

"The one and only," Byron said, cocking his head confidently.

"I am Tenii, son of Pairton. We've been in search of you," Tenii said with a bow.

"Yes, I know. We received your message two days ago and came to cut you off. It looks like we stepped in just in time."

Petra blushed and looked toward the ground.

Dantin looked upon the dwarf with awe. Byron didn't look much taller than Dantin himself was, but Dantin was sure he'd never seen anyone look quite so powerful. The dwarf's long, mangled hair was tied into braids and his dark, leathery skin surrounded strong, squinted eyes and disappeared behind a scruffy beard.

"These are my brothers Lentry and Midcraft," Byron continued. "And I presume that this young man is our lost prince, Dantin." Byron stepped forward and bowed to the prince. His companions did the same until all three had their beards in the dirt.

"Rise, rise." Dantin shook his head as his face reddened. "Why don't you just shake my hand?"

"Whatever you say, sire," Byron laughed and took Dantin's hand in his own weathered hand, feeling as if he could crush every bone with a simple squeeze.

"This is Petra," Dantin said after he had shaken all three dwarves' hands and did his best not to show the pain in his own hand.

Petra stepped forward and bowed to the dwarves.

"Thank you for saving my life. If you hadn't stepped in, I'd be a goner."

"Companions of the prince are protected like the prince. But enough talk, we have to move," Byron said. "Sarpene surely has more spies in the area."

Dantin's ears perked up and he looked around.

"I've had that feeling all day. I thought we were being followed."

"Well," Lentry spoke for the first time. "That was probably Midcraft. We have been following you for a few hours, but he is about as quiet as an elephant in the woods."

"I'm as quiet as an elephant?" Midcraft defended. "You're the one who was spotted. You move like a slug, and have the smell of one, too."

Dantin's eyes met Tenii's and the two smiled at the squabble. This is exactly how Dantin pictured he would have argued if he'd had brothers of his own. The dwarves approached each other until their beards and bellies touched. Dantin was reminded of a coach and an umpire belly-bumping after a bad call. He wondered if they would kick dirt at each other.

"Be careful," Lentry warned with a reddening face. "You may lose your beard in your sleep."

"Then you would lose your head while you were awake."

"Alright, Alright," Byron interrupted. "That's enough. As I said, we have to move quickly."

The dwarves continued to stare each other down.

"And besides," Byron continued. "You both sound like elephants and smell like slugs."

The whole company laughed and eased the tension. The bickering dwarves chuckled and shook their heads as they looked at their older brother.

"That's fine, Byron," Lentry followed. "But we all know who was blessed with good looks in this family." He stood tall and puffed out his chest.

"Yeah, me," Midcraft broke in. "We all know who mother loved best." The whole group laughed again until Tenii brought them back to their task.

"Where do we need to go?" he asked.

"I have a shelter about half a day's journey that way." He pointed in the direction of Kudosh. "It was taken over by the Badlands, but it is well hidden and heavily guarded. No spy could ever find it and no warrior of Sarpene would dare attack it unless they brought a whole army with them."

"Do you have any food, I'm getting tired of these bugs," Dantin asked.

"Of course, Your Majesty, we have the best food for hundreds of miles," Byron answered. "That is how my brothers have grown such nice bellies."

"Yes," Lentry said with a sly smile. "But we all know that you have a few extra chins hidden underneath that beard."

"Perhaps I do," Byron answered amidst the chuckles of everyone else. "Let's go eat."

"That's the best command I've heard in weeks," Petra said.

Midcraft put his arm around the deer.

"Me too, my young friend."

As they traveled, Tenii and Byron walked ahead and discussed the events of the last few days. The other four laughed and joked close behind them. Yet, high up above them, another unseen creature circled. But instead of flying away to alert others, he followed them closely all the way into Kudosh.

15

Hideout

The trip to Byron's shelter in Kudosh went by uneventfully. Though they never left the Badlands, the scenery changed as they traveled. The trees grew denser and much larger, but strangely it seemed to get less dreary. Occasionally Dantin would see a small creature scurry in the distance and he even heard the chirp of a few birds.

"Midcraft, how do we know these animals we see are on our side? Couldn't they be spies of Sarpene?" he asked.

"No, Your Majesty, they are part of our alarm system. We are very close to our dwelling and those creatures would alert us of anything foreign in the area."

"But if we're still in the Badlands, I don't understand how you are not discovered by Sarpene's spies."

"As Byron said, it is very well hidden," Lentry broke in. "Besides, the Badlands did not always extend this far. Patrols have not yet been set here."

"What happens when they do patrol the area?" Petra asked. "Will you be discovered then?"

The dwarves looked at each other and laughed deeply from their stomachs.

"Don't worry about us, my young friends," Midcraft said. "It would have to be a pretty hefty patrol to come near our home. Otherwise, they will be destroyed before they get within half a mile."

Dantin was very interested to see what this dwelling looked like and how many more dwarves were there. He could feel his confidence grow and the fear he'd felt ever since they left Tenii's meadow was slightly eased.

After a while longer, Lentry spoke again.

"Now we're very close. Look up ahead. Can you see anything?"

Petra and Dantin both scanned the area. Dantin saw a dark figure straight ahead, but he strained his eyes and decided it was only a couple of boulders.

"I can't see anything," Petra said after a few seconds.

"Neither can I," said Dantin.

"Exactly," the dwarves said in unison.

It looked to Dantin as if they were approaching the boulders. Tenii and Byron reached the boulders and stopped and waited for the others. As they approached, Byron spoke.

"So what do you think of our home?"

Again Dantin scanned the entire area, but could see nothing that could constitute a well-guarded shelter.

"Um, it's—nice, I guess."

Byron's large belly jiggled as he laughed.

"You are too kind, young prince. But you haven't seen anything yet."

Byron reached in between the boulders and pulled a hidden lever. The smaller of the boulders rumbled and moved to the left, leaving a wooden door. Byron pulled it open and revealed a staircase. Lentry leaned forward and whispered in Dantin's ear.

"Now you see why we are not discovered."

The company entered the dark stairwell and followed it around many bends. Tenii lit up his finger to guide their way through the darkness. Finally, they came to a large metal door. Carved into it was the picture of a very majestic-looking dwarf wearing a crown.

"That is King Sorpius. In ancient times, the dwarves had their own kingdom and he was the most powerful king in all of dwarfish history," Tenii whispered to Dantin and Petra.

Dantin was amazed at the detail of the carving. There stood just the face of the king, but he was surrounded by rays of the sun and accompanied by many trees and weapons, mostly battleaxes. Yet even though it was only a carving, the eyes of the king were very confident and powerful.

Byron reached forward and touched one of the trees on the door. With a great rumble, it pulled back and revealed a large, well-lit room.

"Now this is our home," he said with a smile.

Dantin entered and was astonished. It looked like the inside of a castle from one of his favorite books. Colorful draperies hung from the ceiling, followed by many paintings, mostly of very peculiar-looking dwarves. In the center of the room stood a great statue. It looked like the same dwarf from the door. He stood tall (for a dwarf) with one hand on the hilt of a large, double-edged axe and the other on his hip. Staring straight ahead, the statue looked as though it was a warning of danger for anyone who was not a friend.

"This is amazing," Dantin said very quietly. He walked around the room and examined all the paintings and felt the silky tapestries.

"This is all underground?" he asked.

"Of course," Byron explained. "We are about fifty feet below the surface. When Sarpene took over, this was only a small abandoned mine. We re-opened it and it has become the perfect hiding place."

"But there are no other dwarves. I thought you had an army," Petra said.

"My friends," Lentry said, "this is only the beginning. You haven't seen anything yet."

The dwarves led them through another set of doors and down a long hallway decorated similarly to the room they just left. At the end, it opened into one of the largest rooms Dantin had ever seen. The ceiling sloped up another twenty feet and they stood on top of a large staircase that went down an additional fifty feet at least. At the bottom there sat a long table filled with food. Around it sat a small band of twelve dwarves, lost in a heated discussion.

"I've spent enough time hiding underground like a snake," yelled one of the dwarves. "We can attack and get our own homes back."

"We are not ready to attack. We'll be overrun and all will be lost," pleaded a much older-looking dwarf with a big red hat and a long white beard that looked like it was groomed every day.

Dwarves on both sides of the argument continued to yell back and forth, but in their anger they didn't forget about the food and drink in front of them. When a dwarf wasn't yelling and arguing, it was because he had a mouth full of food, but many times, that didn't even stop them. However, they were intent enough not to notice the visitors until Byron spoke up.

"Brothers, brothers. Is this not the same argument we have had each night for the last ten years? I have brought visitors."

All twelve heads turned at once and stared in silence at the three visitors. A dwarf in the back broke the silence.

"Yeah, a good bit of help they look like they could be. What do we have, a fawn, a young boy, and perhaps the oddest-looking dwarf I've ever seen."

The whole company of dwarves laughed aloud. Dantin's face grew red with embarrassment and both he and Petra looked to the ground. Tenii's face grew red with anger.

"I'll have you know that before you stands the Prince of Pangadesh and the son of the only wizard powerful enough to continue resisting Sarpene after death. Any who doubt our ability or our lineage can step forward now and be relieved of his limbs." Tenii's hand was on the hilt of his sword as he spoke and he even seemed to grow a few inches.

The laughing immediately stopped and the dwarf that had insulted them sank back into his chair and struggled to swallow his mouth full of food. Byron laughed and stepped forward.

"I will vouch for all three of them, both on their lineage and their abilities. This is Tenii, son of Pairton." Tenii bowed, but still did not take his hand off the hilt of his sword.

"This is Petra. He is a spy whose bravery has already been shown." Petra bowed as well and wondered what Byron was talking about.

"And this, my friends, is our prince. Tenii returned him to us. With him is the most famous sword in our kingdom, forged a thousand years ago by our ancestors. Though he may be a boy, he holds his sword stronger than most men I've seen." Dantin was now very embarrassed. He prayed the dwarves would not see his shaking knees as he bowed.

"Come," Lentry broke in. "Let us eat and discuss all this later." He put a hand on Dantin's shoulder and led him to the table. One of the closer dwarves immediately jumped up out of his seat and offered it to the prince.

"Here, Your Majesty, take my chair."

"No-no, you keep it," Dantin said. "I am fine standing."

"No you're not," Midcraft said. "All three of our guests must sit and rest from their long journey."

Two other dwarves left their seats and offered them to the visitors with a bow.

"Thank you," Tenii said, returning their bow and finally let go of his sword's hilt.

Byron took his seat at the head of the table and Midcraft and Lentry took theirs to the left of him. The food on the table was incredible. There were breads, rolls, pastries, pies, fruits, potatoes and many other things Dantin did not recognize, and there wasn't a single insect in sight.

While they ate, Tenii told the dwarves of all their adventures up to that point. Both Dantin and Petra received many congratulations on their bravery. Two of the dwarves even offered to help Tenii complete Dantin's training. As his stomach got full, Dantin's eyes got increasingly heavy. Around him, the dwarves resumed their argument about when and how to attack Sarpene, but Dantin was falling asleep where he sat.

"Your Majesty," Byron said when he saw Dantin's head bobbing, "come, I have a place where you can rest."

Byron got up from the table and led Dantin, Petra, and Tenii to a dark room. Inside there were three cots.

"You can sleep without being disturbed in here," he said. But the only thing Dantin heard was the bed calling his name. He stumbled to the edge and plopped down, falling asleep almost before he hit the cot. Tenii and Petra did the same and all three were out before Byron had even left the room. He gave them one last look and closed the door behind him.

16

Attack

"How did I surround myself with the world's biggest IDIOTS?!" The scream rumbled through the castle, scattering everyone who heard. Two hyenas didn't get out of the way in time and the sorcerer vaporized them with a flash from his finger.

"MOTH, GET IN HERE!"

The gnome sighed and slowly emerged from the closet.

"Y-yes, sire."

"I was just told by your spy that your patrol of wolves was wiped out in less than two minutes and that all three of the intruders survived."

"But, sire, that's impossi—"

"He also told me that three dwarves were involved, and they led a boy, a deer, and another dwarf into Kudosh."

Moth grew pale and knew his life was about to come to an end, but he wasn't going down without a fight.

"Please, master. Please spare me." Tears streamed down his face and he fell to his knees, clutching Sarpene's robes. "I'll do anything, you name it, just don't kill me."

"Don't touch me, you twit." Sarpene kicked the gnome and sent him rolling backwards. "The only reason you're still alive now is that your spy actually did something right. He followed the intruders into Kudosh."

"That's good, that's good. We'll send another patrol to get—"

"NO! This time I will go myself."

Moth stood with his mouth gaping.

"Uh, sire. I don't know if that's a good idea. We don't know what to expect in Kudosh. And besides, it's too far from the castle, your powers will diminish."

"Do you think that I cannot destroy each one of these cowardly rebels with my bare hands?" Sarpene's eyes glared bright red.

"No, sire, I just—"

"Careful, worm," Sarpene warned as the tip of his finger began to glow.

"As you wish, sire." The gnome stepped back and bowed.

"Good. Send word to every wolf, hyena, giant, and anything else that may be in the area. Have them meet me outside of Kudosh. How long will that take?"

"Well, it shouldn't take more than a couple weeks, a month tops," Moth said, counting on his fingers.

"You have three days."

"Three days?"

"Problem?"

The gnome gulped and took off out the door.

"Nope, no problem," he called back as he exited.

Dantin awoke and stretched his arms above his head in a huge yawn. Smiling, he marveled at the looseness of his muscles. This was his first pain-free wake up in weeks. He reached down and touched the soft mattress he'd been sleeping on and nodded his head.

Tenii and Petra were still sleeping, so he carefully made his way to the door and followed the torch-lit corridor to the humongous room they had eaten in the night before. There, he found all the dwarves arguing again.

"How long must we wait?" called a young-looking dwarf.

"Patience, Argo," answered Ebulum, the elderly dwarf with the white beard and red hat from the day before. "When the time comes to attack we will know it."

"There were wolves less than ten miles from here," another joined in. "How can we continue to wait? We're going to be discovered sooner or later, and I'd rather go down fighting than let them take my home again."

"If we move forward and attack too soon and we are beaten, then our home will be lost anyway. There will be no one left to defend it."

The argument continued in this fashion for a very long time. Strangely, Byron never joined in. He simply sat at the head of the table with his hairy chin upon his folded hands, listening to every word. Midcraft and Lentry weren't shy about choosing sides. "It felt great to fight a wolf again," Lentry said.

"Aye, it made me feel thirty years younger," Midcraft added. "I'm ready to go find a few more right now."

"And we may just get that chance," another agreed. "If wolves were that close yesterday, then perhaps tomorrow there will be many more. My axe is ready to take skins."

"If you are right, then we must stay and defend our home, not run off looking for trouble and leaving our home poorly guarded."

Neither side gained much ground. Whenever anyone made a good point, the other side made an equally good point and they were right back where they started. It was actually very frustrating to watch. But still, Byron said nothing. He didn't even mediate. It seemed as though many of the arguments were directed at him, like he would make the final decision.

A few minutes later, Tenii appeared at Dantin's side.

"Are they still arguing?"

"Yep, they've been at it for a while. I'm not even sure that they haven't been arguing throughout the night."

Tenii shook his head and yawned.

"Well, I'm wondering about food."

"You read my mind again," Dantin said with a smile.

Finally someone at the table noticed them and addressed the three travelers.

"Ah, our visitors have wakened from the dead. Come, come, sit and join in our discussion."

They now had more chairs set out at the table, so no dwarves had to give up their seats. As soon as they were seated, it began again.

"So what do you think, Prince Dantin? Should we attack or should we sit around doing nothing?" asked Argo.

"We're not doing *nothing*," defended the elderly dwarf again. "We are getting ready, training, learning, and growing,"

"Well, all of this training, learning, and growing has made us fat and lazy."

Byron finally spoke.

"Let the prince speak. Where do your thoughts lie?"

Tenii spoke first.

"Dantin's training is not yet fini—"

"Hold on, Tenii, let the boy speak," Byron interrupted.

Everyone looking at him and waiting for a decision suddenly embarrassed Dantin. Both sides of the argument spun around in his head and grasping for one didn't seem possible. But one point that hadn't been made popped into his head and made the decision for him.

"The longer we wait, the more dangerous it becomes for my parents. Tenii tells me that they have already grown old and weak. I would rather die trying to free them than to arrive too late."

"You do know that if the king or queen dies the powers of the kingdom pass into you," Byron pointed out. "That is a lot of power, if power is what you are looking for."

"NO!" Dantin shook the table with a slamming fist. "I don't care about power. I want a mother and a father, not a kingdom, and I'm trying really hard not to fault you for asking that." Dantin looked away.

"I apologize, Your Majesty, I did not mean to upset you," Byron said with a bow. Then he addressed the rest of the room.

"The prince wishes to rescue his parents. What do you think about that?"

The same arguments began once again. Dantin stood and stomped off. Byron began to follow, but Tenii stopped him.

"No, Byron, I'll go to him. You make them make a decision." Tenii turned and followed Dantin down the long hallway.

"Dantin, wait."

Dantin's fists were clenched white. He stopped at Tenii's request, but he did not turn. He continued to stare down the long hallway. When Tenii caught up, it looked as though Dantin was ready to put his fist through the wall.

"Why, Tenii, why? Why do they argue so? Don't they care if the king and queen die?"

"I'm afraid that is the nature of dwarves, young Dantin. But I assure you, once they come to a decision, every dwarf will stick to it at all costs."

"Well, what if they decide to do nothing?"

"Then we will seek aid elsewhere. Dwarves are not the only ones left who oppose Sarpene."

"Why is it such a tough decision? Why can't they just help?"

"Again, I'm afraid it is the nature of dwarves to think of themselves first. We must remember that if we are to convince them. There has to be something in it for them."

"What about you? You're part dwarf and you're not like that."

Tenii smiled.

"I wasn't raised among other dwarves. My mother was very special with a kind heart. I was raised to serve others."

"And what of Byron?"

"If we are to convince the others, it'll be through Byron. He is different from the others. I sense compassion from him, which is very strange from a full-blood dwarf. I think he wants to help us."

"Then why doesn't he just tell the others to help as well? He is the leader, isn't he?"

"Let's just hope he can influence them."

Dantin and Tenii made their way back to the main room, but they found all the dwarves scrambling around.

"What's going on?" Tenii asked as he grabbed Midcraft.

"Our decision may have been made for us, there are intruders above."

Giving each other a quick look, Dantin and Tenii took off to retrieve their weapons. When they returned, they found Byron giving orders.

"Lentry, take five others with you and head to the back entrance. Your Majesty, you're with me."

"Alright," Lentry yelled, looking around. "Who's with me?"

Five dwarves stepped forward and all six took off toward back of the cave. While the remaining defenders went over their positions, Petra showed up from the back room.

"What's happening?" he yawned sleepily.

"Intruders," Dantin answered.

"Petra," Byron began. "I need you to stay down here. It's going to be dangerous up there."

"But how can I stay—"

"Everybody else, let's go!" He did not wait for a response.

Dantin's eyes gave Petra a quick apology and he followed the dwarves up the stairs.

"What's up there, Byron?" he asked as he got to the front.

"I don't know, but whatever they are, there are a lot of them."

Dantin took a deep breath and looked toward Tenii.

"We have some work to do, my friend."

Tenii nodded solemnly and added, "How long do you think it'll be before Petra disobeys Byron as well?"

"I'll give him five minutes," Dantin said with a smile. "Any longer and he'll die from anticipation."

The company finally reached the outside door and Byron stopped them.

"Whatever is outside is trying to take our home from us. I'll die before that happens."

Byron's comments were met with grunts and cheers of agreement from the entire company.

"Good, then let's go."

Outside the caves was even drearier than it had been the day before. Dantin's heart raced a mile a minute. He gripped and re-gripped his sword over and over again. Following Byron closely, he scanned the entire area, but could find nothing out of the ordinary.

"Spread out," Byron whispered. "There's something out here, I can feel it."

Dantin looked back at Tenii and shrugged his shoulders. The two of them moved off to the left and crouched behind a large bush.

"There's nothing out here," Dantin began. "I think it was a false—"

"Shhhh, listen," Tenii urged. "There's something here."

Dantin listened and looked as hard as he could, but he couldn't even hear the dwarves moving around.

"Where is everyone?"

Dantin nearly jumped out of his skin as he spun and lifted his sword to find Petra standing right behind him. Tenii almost struck him even after he realized who had startled them.

"Petra, what are you doing here!?" Tenii scolded as Dantin sighed and laughed.

"I'm not staying down there alone while you're up here fighting without me," Petra said puffing out his chest.

"I wondered how long it would take you," Dantin smiled, shaking his head and turning to scan the area again. This time he caught movement out of the corner of his eye.

"Tenii, left," he called, but it was gone. Things didn't look or feel the same. His chest felt heavy with anticipation. Suddenly, a whistling sound came out of nowhere. He caught another glance at something, this time to the right, then to the left, and straight ahead. The shadows looming above in the trees began to scatter, some even falling to the ground.

"Over there, no, there. No, now it's there." He pointed all around, but as soon as he looked directly at anything, it would vanish. "What is all this?"

"I have no clue." Tenii spoke in a hoarse whisper and shook his head. "But I think we're surrounded."

"By what?"

"I'm not sure, but I think it's—"

—WHAM!

Dantin watched with horror-filled eyes as Tenii's legs gave out and his limp body splattered to the ground like a raindrop.

"TENII!"

As he frantically reached for his friend an explosion of creatures came from all around and arrows filled the air, one hitting the ground just between his feet. Crouching and breathing a sigh of relief as he felt Tenii's pulse, he raised his sword and turned toward Petra.

"Petra, get out of—Petra? Petra, where are you?" Dantin spun around madly searching for the fawn. He looked toward the dwarves, but could see nothing through the swirling shadows and flying arrows. All around he could hear grunts and cries.

"NOOOO!" The scream erupted through his lips as he charged the middle of the swirling shadows, holding his sword above his head, ready to strike.

—WHAM!

Dantin's world darkened as he fell face first into a bush and lost the hilt of the sword.

17

Queen Sylvania

Dantin awoke to another train wreck in his head. Struggling to open his eyes, he wiped them and ran his hands through his hair with a sigh. Trying to figure out where he was and what was going on, he looked around and found himself in a strange room. His headache betrayed the possibility that this was all a dream. From his back, he noticed a light coming into the room brighter than anything he had seen in many days. Rolling over, he pushed himself to his feet with great effort, letting go of a groan that filled the air. But the effort was too much for the explosion in his head and he fell to a knee with his head throbbing between his hands. After a few of seconds he made another try.

Steadying himself, he worked his way to the window that was letting in all the light. Strangely, his legs did not seem to want to work by themselves. Each step was a struggle against the aching insisting he lie down. Reaching the window, he looked back and saw that he had traveled merely ten steps, though it had seemed like ten miles through a thick forest. As he peered out the window, the pain momentarily subsided, leaving him basking in the most beautifully warm sunshine. Dantin hadn't seen the sky since the meadow outside Tenii's house and this was quite possibly the most wonderful thing he had ever seen. It looked like he could see for thousands of miles through the dazzling blue sky. Puffy clouds taking the innocent shapes of small creatures and flowers rolled through, but the sun fought its way through, not letting them cover its magnificence. Dantin's next look was down, and the dizziness returned. The ground was nowhere to be found through the thousands of treetops far below. He looked up and found that he was in a tree himself, towering above every other in the forest.

"Feeling better?" The voice nearly shot Dantin through the roof. He spun and reached for the hilt of the sword that wasn't there. Before him stood a beautiful creature that looked like a small woman with long, perfectly braided black hair that hung to the middle of her back and green eyes that cheered up the room more than the sun coming through the window.

"Wh-who are you?" he choked out when his startled heart began beating again.

"I am Sylvania, Queen of the elflands, and you are in my kingdom." Her sweet voice soothed Dantin's heart and strangely calmed him down, leaving him too bewildered to say anything else.

"And you, I am guessing, are the long-lost Prince Dantin of Pangadesh?"

Dantin managed a confused nod.

"Welcome."

"Where are my friends?" Dantin asked as he began to regain his head.

"Your companions are not here, we only took you."

"Took me?" Dantin's hands went back to his head. The throbbing wouldn't allow him to bring his thoughts together. "What do you mean took me? What do you want with me?"

"Do not worry, you are in no danger here." The queen walked to the window and breathed the sweet air in with a deep breath. "We brought you here to keep you safe."

"Safe from what? I was safe with Byron and Tenii."

"Not for much longer, Sarpene now knows of the dwarves and their dwelling."

"How do you know that?"

"Sarpene is not the only one with spies. We keep track of everything that goes on in the forest."

"But I don't need protected by you. The dwarves wouldn't have let anything happen to me."

"Then why were *we* able to get to you so easily?"

"I-I don't know." He staggered a little. "I need to sit down."

Falling to a knee, he buried his head in his hands again. It felt as though it weighed a thousand pounds.

"Here," the queen stepped forward and held out her hand and produced a green leaf. "Eat this, it will quiet your head."

Dantin took the leaf from her soft hand, examined it for a second, and popped it in his mouth. Almost instantly his head cleared a little and the headache subsided. Within a minute he was able to stand again more steadily.

"Better?" she asked.

"Yes, thank you." Dantin's brow furrowed. "What is it?"

"A special herb that grows in our kingdom."

With his head clear now, Dantin was able to look at the queen's face more closely and he saw that she was not a woman. She was very small with soft features, skin almost as white as the clouds he'd just seen, and long, pointed ears even bigger than his own. But her most distinguishing feature was piercing eyes that seemed to hold a great deal of wisdom among their beauty.

"What are you?"

"What am I?" she repeated with a smile.

"No, I'm sorry. I didn't mean to be rude; it's just that I'm still confused about this whole world."

"No need to apologize. But of all creatures, you should be able to recognize what I am, for I am much like you."

Dantin looked again, even closer this time.

"Are you an elf?"

The queen smiled again.

"Yes, and I've known you since the day you were born."

The confusion rolled back into Dantin.

"You know me? How?"

"Your mother was my closest friend."

"You know my mother!?" Dantin's voice cracked and he almost choked.

"She and I grew up together. In fact, on the day you were born, you were betrothed to my own daughter, Tierra."

"Betrothed? What's that?"

"It means you were to marry her."

"*Marry* her?" Dantin's face contorted and he wrinkled his nose. "But I'm only a boy, I can't get married."

Sylvania's laugh sounded almost like she were singing, but it did little to calm Dantin this time.

"I'm not going to get married," Dantin repeated.

"Perhaps not now, but someday maybe. For now, you must rest more. The herb will only work for a few hours, after that your headache will return unless you rest. I'll have one of the servants bring you food later this morning."

Dantin's mind was still racing around the marriage idea. He kept thinking back to the girls back at school and how weird he felt around them. He thought about all the games the boys used to play where girls had cooties and the boys would get sick if they touched them. Of course, none of the boys would ever let Dantin play, but he saw them get sick when girls touched them and he also saw how mad the girls got when the boys played. As the queen turned to leave, another thought jumped back into his head.

"Wait. Were my friends in danger too?"

The queen sighed and hesitated before she turned back around.

"Yes, you were all in danger. That is why we had to get you away from there. We cannot allow Sarpene to harm you. It would mean the end of our world."

"Do they know where I am?"

"I'm sure Byron has figured it out by now." An embarrassed smile grew on the queen's face. "He's probably not too happy with us right now—we left him with quite a bump on his head as well."

"None of the dwarves were injured, were they?"

"Nothing that won't heal in a couple of days. Now rest, as I said, I'll send a servant up with some food later."

The queen turned again, but Dantin's mind was still swirling with questions he needed answered.

"Does Sarpene know that you have taken me?" he called to her back. Again the queen hesitated before she turned around.

"No, he thinks you are still with the dwarves." She turned to leave again, and this time, she almost got to the door before Dantin stopped her.

"Wait," he called urgently. "If Sarpene still thinks I'm with the dwarves, isn't he still going to attack them as you said?"

The queen sighed a third time and did not turn back around this time. "Yes, he will attack."

Dantin's stomach turned over and his eyes grew three times their size. "Then we have to go help them."

"That is not possible, Dantin." The queen finally turned and gave him a comforting look. "Dwarves and elves won't fight together. They wouldn't want our help, even if we were willing in the first place."

"Then I need to go help. They are my friends." Dantin's fists clenched up and he again reached for the missing sword.

The queen looked him straight in the eye, then down to the floor before she spoke again.

"Dantin, we cannot let you go anywhere. You are safe here. If Sarpene cannot get to you, then he can do you no harm, and our world is safe."

"No. I'm not going to stay here while my friends are killed. I'm going to help them."

Dantin pushed past the queen to the door himself, but it wouldn't open when he pulled.

"What is this?" he asked angrily.

"Dantin," the queen began more firmly. "You are not going anywhere. As I said, the safety of our world depends on you staying alive."

"Well, the safety of my friends may depend on my help." Dantin's eyes began to well up as he stared directly into the queen's eyes.

"Be that as it may, you cannot leave."

"So I'm a prisoner?"

"You are a guest."

"A guest who cannot leave." Dantin's eyes now burned into the queen's. She closed her eyes and shook her head slowly.

"I'm afraid not." She put a soft hand on his shoulder and he brushed it away and went to the window. He could already feel his head fogging up again.

"I am sorry, Dantin, but it must be this way." Dantin kept staring out the window with his knuckles clenched white. Without another word, the queen turned and left the room. Turning his eyes toward the closed door, Dantin gave it another try, but it wouldn't budge. He was trapped.

18

Battered and Bruised

"Ughh," Tenii groaned. From the ground, he opened his eyes to find himself in complete darkness. His head exploded as he tried to shake the cobwebs loose and he struggled to keep consciousness. After a couple minutes the throbbing lessened. He struggled to his feet and looked around. Above, the dark trees looming over everything swayed in a stale, unrefreshing breeze. The sky was as dark and dull as Tenii had ever seen it. As his eyes adjusted to the blackness his head began to clear enough to put thoughts together. Looking down, he found Dantin's sword lying at his feet. "Dantin!" The barely audible name left his lips and disappeared into the darkness. He noticed a large hump lying on the ground fifteen feet away.

"Dantin," he repeated as he tore forward. Fear and despair drove through him as he reached the shape. He turned it over to find a dwarf with a long, scruffy beard and a lump the size of a baseball on his forehead.

"Midcraft?" he called, but got no answer. Putting his ear to the dwarf's mouth, he felt soft, warm breath escape. Tenii looked up and around and found another body lying not far away. Jumping up, he found it to be Lentry, lying facedown in a bush just as his brother was. Tenii found five more unconscious dwarves lying about, each with lumps on his head and no weapon. All were still alive, but not by very much. Tenii continued searching around, but Dantin was not to be found.

"Dantin," he said in a loud whisper. "Dantin, where are you?"

"He's gone."

The voice nearly jumped Tenii out of his skin. Turning quickly, he saw a battered Byron, standing wearily behind him.

"They took him," Byron said, leaning against a tree.

Tenii's face went blank as his eyes watered up and his lip quivered beneath his beard. His legs turned to rubber and he thumped onto his rear end. His eyes stared wide into the black nothingness that surrounded them.

"Then all is lost," he managed through a spinning head.

"No, not yet," Byron said, struggling to reach Tenii. He put out his short stubby hand and laid it on Tenii's quivering shoulder. "It was not Sarpene who took him."

"What?" Tenii blurted, as if he were suddenly awakened from a trance. "How do you know?"

Byron held up his other hand to produce an arrow. The shaft was split, but the razor sharp point was not touched and the bright green feather gleamed in the darkness. "This arrow was crafted by the elves; the feathers still carry their mark."

Tenii took the arrow and examined it closer. The green feathers were swirled and a tiny black eye sat in the middle of each. "Has Sarpene taken control of the elves now too?" he asked, not letting any hope go to his head.

"No elf would ever work for Sarpene, his magic is too black and impure. The elves' tradition and culture would clash with that of Sarpene's. They would cancel each other out."

"So what are you saying? The elves have Dantin?" Tenii was still having trouble putting his thoughts together. "What would they want with him?"

"I don't know, but the fawn isn't here either." Byron hobbled over to Midcraft and placed his ear against the unconscious dwarf's mouth. Satisfied, he pulled a root out of his pocket and held it under his nose until Midcraft's body jerked. His eyes fluttered open and looked around for a couple seconds, then closed again.

"Midcraft," Byron yelled, frantically shaking his brother.

Midcraft's eyes opened again and he looked up at Byron. "If you don't mind, I was in the middle of a perfectly good dream about Laurine. You're not nearly as pretty as she is." With that, he closed his eyes again and tried to retrieve the dream.

A relieved smile broke through Byron's tough face. "Get up, you twit," he said with a soft kick to Midcraft's side.

Midcraft laughed and sat up with a howl, his hands going straight to his head. "Wow, who hit me with a tree?"

Byron shook his head and attended to his other brother, who woke up with an equally sarcastic remark about Byron's weathered face. In a few minutes, they had found each of the twelve dwarves alive, but not looking well. The beat-up band gathered and sat in a circle and sounded like a group of old ladies complaining about sore hips. Byron explained to the miserable party what he thought happened.

"Elves," Narl, one of the older dwarves, spat, "those nosy little gremlins. Who do they think they are, attacking us?"

The crowd grumbled right along with him, each with one hand clenching an imaginary weapon and the other holding an aching head.

"So what are we going to do about it?" Tenii broke in. "I'm sworn to protect that boy and I'm not going to sit here nursing a headache while he's taken prisoner somewhere."

"I'm sure he's okay," Byron said twisting his beard.

"How do you know that? You were just as unconscious as I was when they took him. And what of Petra, why would they possibly take him? He's of no good to them."

"Maybe they were hungry," Narl said with a chuckle.

Tenii's eyes exploded fiery red. He shot to his feet and momentarily forgot about his aches and pains.

"YOU MONSTER!" he cried, charging at the dwarf. "How could you say that?" The other dwarf was on his feet before Tenii reached him and they hit with a thud, knocking them both back into the darkness, rolling and punching the whole way. The rest of the party was on their feet cheering almost before the two hit and they had a circle built faster than any middle school brawl. The two rumbled around for a few seconds before Byron broke through like thunder.

"STOP!!!" He grabbed Lentry by the back of the collar and drug him into the circle. They jumped on the dwarves and yanked them apart. Byron laid on Tenii and Lentry on Narl, but the two were still clutching and screaming toward each other.

"Enough!" Byron screamed. "We can't do this!"

After a few seconds, Tenii calmed down enough for Byron to hold him without effort and he began to weep. Narl relaxed soon after and the circled crowd quieted and just watched. Byron angrily pushed off of Tenii and turned in a circle, looking each of the dwarves in the eyes.

"The elves took Dantin for a reason. That means that we must be in danger, and we're fighting each other!" He threw his hands in the air and broke through the circle again, grumbling to himself as he thumped away.

Tenii sat up and saw each dwarf looking down toward the ground. He looked at Narl, who was doing the same.

"I'm sorry, my friend," he said sheepishly. "I don't know what came over me."

Narl didn't respond. In fact, he didn't even look up. After an awkward silence, Midcraft broke in.

"Hey, we're all on edge here. Let's just relax and figure out what we need to do."

Narl kicked the ground and slowly looked up. His eyes met Tenii's for a split second and a quiet "sorry" came out. He then turned around and moved to the outside of the circle.

"Alright," Midcraft said. "Now let's get back to the cave, Byron will join us shortly."

Without words, the group of dwarves trudged through the darkness to the hidden door. Byron continued walking around trying to calm himself down and figure out what to do. As Tenii reached the door, he stopped and spotted Byron about twenty yards away. Tenii broke the line and headed toward the troubled dwarf.

"What did you mean about trouble?" he asked as he reached Byron's side.

Byron sighed and waited a few seconds before any words came out of his mouth.

"The elves had to have cause to attack us and take the prince. Their spies are more clever and sneaky than ours are. Something must be going on that we don't know about."

"But it's a secret cave, what could be happening?"

Byron laughed and shook his head.

"If the elves knew where we are, then Sarpene might as well."

"Then we have to leave. We have to go after Dantin and Petra."

Byron looked away and stroked his beard.

"You know, it's not going to be easy to convince the others to leave the cave for a rescue mission."

Tenii's face sunk. He'd forgotten how stubborn the dwarves were. His hand mimicked Byron's as he tried to figure it out. After a few silent minutes, his eyes lit up and he spoke again.

"Tell them we seek revenge, they'll go for that."

Byron thought about it for a couple seconds and then began to nod his head to himself.

"But what happens when we get there—our small band cannot defeat the elves and all their enchantments."

"We won't have to," Tenii's eyes brightened up like a child's on Christmas day. "When we get close, you and I will act as spies and look for Dantin and Petra. If we can find them and bring them out, we simply have to flee."

"If the others are after revenge, they won't flee."

"If you flee, they'll flee."

"And if we can't find the prince or the fawn, what then?"

Tenii hesitated.

"Then we attack and take our chances."

Byron's head cocked to the side at last suggestion. He looked hard into Tenii's narrow eyes and shuddered as he agreed.

"Alright, I'll go talk to the others."

Tenii nodded and Byron was off. Turning around, Tenii looked up through the large trees and caught a glimpse of the dark sky.

"Hang in there, buddy," he said aloud. "We're coming for you."

19

Prison Escape

"Ow, ow, come on, slow down." Sprinting through the dark woods, Petra dodged as many obstacles as possible, but still ran face first into branches and stepped into holes that sent him sprawling. The events of the night kept playing over and over in his head, pushing him to run faster and hold back tears. It was quite possibly the scariest thing he'd ever seen, outside of the wolves, that is.

He had quietly escaped from the cave and was looking around for the intruders. The air felt different somehow, heavy and still. Petra looked hard through the trees for the sun, but he couldn't come up with it. He stood alone in the dark wood, straining his eyes and ears for any movement or change, hoping there was nothing looming in the darkness behind him.

Something wasn't right, his skin began to crawl and each of his tiny hairs stood straight up. His eyes adjusted and he finally spotted a slight movement and heard Dantin's voice, followed by Tenii hushing him. He remembered watching Tenii fall, and out of nowhere, hundreds of creatures fell from the sky, accompanied by thousands of arrows. An arrow glanced Petra's shoulder and stuck into the tree, sending him to the ground falling through a bush. Screaming, he felt for a gaping hole and an arrow sticking from his chest, but found only a scratch on his shoulder. After a few moments, he regained his head and noticed the forest had fallen silent again. Popping his head up, he scanned the area and it was empty.

"DANTIN!" he screamed, bursting up. He ran to where he'd seen Dantin and Tenii, but found only Tenii lying unconscious.

"Dantin, where are you!?" Petra scanned the entire area and ran about, finding many dwarves, some unconscious and others writhing in pain, but none seemed to be seriously injured, so he continued searching all around, fighting back tears.

—Snap.

Petra perked his ears and froze, unsure of the direction of the sound.

—Snap.

With this one, Petra's eyes shot skyward. As he strained, he caught a glimpse of the leaves and branches above and saw them swaying slightly. He could see the dull outline of the sky.

"The trees!" Petra said aloud to himself. He bolted forward to a spot where it seemed particularly empty and looked up. He was just in time to catch a shadow bolt through. The fawn watched for a few seconds and found other dark shapes that leaped from tree to tree like flying squirrels looking for nuts. Not even thinking, he took off in the same direction.

Hours later and Petra was feeling every bump, bruise, and scrape from the hunt. He had lost the shadows some time ago, but they had moved in a straight line up until that point, so he continued.

"Cursed creatures, doesn't evil rest?" The annoyed deer continued, stopping only to pick himself from the ground or to regain his thoughts and objective.

"Keep going, come on." He hoofed himself in the side of the head, shook out the cobwebs and continued. As he traveled, the forest brightened. It was like a slow dawn, getting lighter with every hour. The trees looked less gloomy and the foul stench was sweetened by a soft breeze.

"HALT!"

Petra froze in place, too afraid to breathe. Two arrows whizzed by either side of him and stuck in the ground.

"If you move, the next one will stick from your chest."

Shooting straight up, Dantin again had to break through a fog of confusion. With a shake he found the headache to be gone, yet he had to struggle to remember where he was. A knock on the door jolted his heart and sent his hand to his swordless hip. As the door slowly opened, the sun itself seemed to enter. Veiled in garments whiter than the freshest snow, a young elf glided though the open door and stopped in front of him with eyes sparkling brighter then the closest star. Her pale skin seemed to glow just as her garments, yet held the slightest pink tint above her dimples and smile that belonged to an angel. Dantin's jaw dropped to the floor and cotton filled his mouth as if he'd been hiking in the desert. He became self-conscious and was sure that she could hear his heart pounding through his chest.

"I am Princess Tierra, Your Majesty, daughter of Sylvania." With a perfect curtsy, her eyes grazed Dantin's for a split second before falling to his feet.

The only sounds that came from Dantin's mouth were much like that of a cat hacking up a hairball. His eyes glazed over and remained fastened. They both stood silently for what seemed like hours before Sylvania spoke again.

"D-did they bring you dinner?"

Dantin managed to nod his head slightly and the elf's eyes met his for another second. She ripped them away and found the cold plate of food sitting under the window. Silence again seemed to separate the two like a brick wall. Dantin finally caught his head enough to realize his awkward stare and his eyes too fell to the floor.

"We have another prisoner," Sylvania blurted.

"What?" Dantin was broken of his trance. "Who?"

"A young fawn who claims to be your servant."

"Petra! Take me to him."

Tierra stuttered and shook her head.

"I-I can't do that. I'm not even supposed to be here."

Dantin's eyes glared.

"I don't care. Take me to him, now."

Tierra's shyness wore off just as quickly as Dantin's had.

"Excuse me?" Her eyes raised and bored right through his. "Don't give *me* orders. If I'm not mistaken, you are a prisoner yourself."

"I'm no more a prisoner than he should be. Go tell your mommy to let us both go."

A look of disbelief filled the young elf's face and this time *her* mouth fell open.

"I-I could have you hung."

"Oh yeah, like I said, why don't you ask your mommy why I'm a prisoner here. She has no right to keep me."

"My mother is the queen, and she can lock you up for spitting on the ground if she pleases."

Dantin turned his head and spit on the wall.

"Good, now go tell her she can keep me here forever."

Tierra was horrified. It was her turn to hack up a hairball.

"I-I—if you had any sense about you, you'd kneel down and—."

"Well, it's a good thing I don't have any sense or I'd toss you out of here on your head."

"Errrrr." The elf spun and stomped out of the room, slamming the back end of her gown in the door. Dantin laughed as he heard a loud rip and saw the cloth remain as he heard the princess stomp away. As soon as the sound faded away, Dantin was at the window looking down again. He couldn't see the ground through the thick trees below, but there was a ledge about twenty feet below that could give him a better view of what was below.

Scanning the room, Dantin looked for anything to help him lower himself to the ledge. He remembered old prison movies when inmates would make a rope out of bed sheets to climb down, but he also remembered one where the sheets broke apart and dropped the prisoners thirty or forty feet to the ground. Remembering how far the drop would be for him, he swallowed the lump that had formed in his throat. Shaking the thought from his head, he searched the room for anything to help. There was no bed, so of course there were no sheets, and the mat he slept on wasn't going to help either. Scurrying around the room, he could find nothing helpful. He was just about to give up hope when his toe caught on something and sent him sprawling.

"Grrr," Dantin spat, slamming his hands onto the ground and looking around at what tripped him. A coiled rug lay behind him beneath a glass table. He spun over and examined it closer. It seemed to be made from tightly spun blue and red thread, coiled into a circle.

"That's it," Dantin said to himself with a smile. He found where the coil started and pulled with all his might, but the rug wouldn't give.

"COME ON!" he groaned through his teeth, straining again until he felt as if his eyes were going to pop out.

With no luck, he threw the rug to the ground and kicked at the table, shattering it against the wall. Slumping to the ground, Dantin put his head in his hands and calmed himself down. With a sigh he shook his head and leaned back, putting his hand right on a shard of glass.

"OWW!" he screamed, grabbing his wrist and watching as the dark red blood trickled over his hand and down his forearm. Just as he began to lash out again, he stopped suddenly and looked at the broken glass lying around the floor. Forgetting his cut, he jumped up, found a large piece with a sharp edge, and returned to the rug. Smiling and shaking his head at his temper bringing him luck, he started sawing at the edge of the rug with the glass

Slowly, the rug began to unravel. His forearms burned from the constant motion, and he had to stop momentarily to wrap his bleeding hand with a curtain, but Dantin persisted, thinking of his friend trapped somewhere in this castle and Tenii somewhere in the woods, about to be ambushed by Sarpene. He figured that he needed about twenty feet of rope, so he cut forty feet, making sure not to leave himself dangling hundreds of feet in the air. After about forty-five minutes, he had cut himself enough.

Looking down at his hands, he found tiny cuts on each of his fingertips from his makeshift blade, but pushing that from his mind, he went back to the window and looked down. The twenty feet now looked like two hundred and he wondered how he would hold on. Remembering the prison movies again, he knotted the rope every five feet so he could get a better grip.

Now all Dantin had to do was find an anchor, something strong enough to hold his weight. His heart sank. The room was empty and the wooden window frame gave way with a slight kick. He sat down again to think, wondering if he should throw another fit—the last one gave him his last answer. As frustration set in again, he went to the door and began slamming his fists.

"LET ME OUT OF HERE!" Grabbing the knob with both hands, Dantin pulled and kicked at the same time. After a few seconds, he stopped suddenly again, coming to another realization. He looked down at the doorknob and gave another stiff tug, but the door didn't even shudder. Bringing the rope over, he tied another knot and fastened it to the knob. Tugging it to make sure it was secure, he turned and threw the other end of the rope through the window and looked down again. The rope hung at least five feet past the window below.

Rubbing his hands together and gathering his courage, Dantin readied himself. He climbed onto the windowsill and slowly let himself down, holding the rope with one hand and the window with the other. Wondering whether the rope and anchor would hold his weight, he took a deep breath and let go of the window, securing his feet on the closest knot down from him and holding with both hands on the knot by his head. Feeling secure, he slowly let himself down to the next knot. The rope burned in his hands, but not even the most excruciating pain could make him lose his grip. He continued in the same manner to the next knot.

"Don't look down, just don't look down," Dantin coached himself, but he still couldn't help it. His eyes fell to the distance below and thoughts of falling screamed through his head, causing his world to spin.

"Nice, you idiot," Dantin scolded himself, closing his eyes and hugging the rope with all his might. A few deep breaths calmed his nauseous stomach and he willed himself to lower another knot, this time *without* looking down. One quick glance to the window below told him he only had one knot to go before he could stand on the windowsill. With another deep breath, he lowered himself again, just enough for his toes to catch the edge.

With a final slide, the fire building within his hands almost got the better of him, sending him through the leaves to whatever lay below. He kicked at the window and it gave a little. He tried a little more weight behind his kick and the wooden frame cracked. With a final swing, he threw all his weight against the frame and let go of the rope, crashing into the room.

20

Trapped

"I'm not going after hundreds of elves to save a boy and a deer," Narl's comment was accompanied by grumbles of agreement from many of the dwarves.

"That boy may be our world's only chance," Tenii broke in. "If Sarpene gets him, there will be no stopping him."

"But *our* world was fine without him. He's the one who brought the wolves to us and he's the reason my head's pounding."

"Then why not go and give the elves a few headaches," Lentry added, bringing grumbles of agreement as well.

"Why don't we forget the boy and go directly after Sarpene." Shooting up, Argo held his battered axe above his head. "If he is safe with the elves, why bring him back into danger."

The argument continued in circles with everyone shouting different opinions. As usual, Byron simply sat back and observed the chaos, waiting.

"Won't Sarpene simply go after the elves?" Lentry asked.

"No," Tenii spoke up. "Sarpene wouldn't dare venture there. It's too far away from the castle in Pangadesh."

"What does that have to do with it?" one of the dwarves called.

"His power is stolen, and because the true king is still alive, he cannot travel far from the castle without losing powers. That is why the Badlands only extend so far, that is the stretch of his power right now."

"What happens if the boy dies and Sarpene kills the king?" Avrom asked, not sure he wanted to hear the answer.

Tenii sighed.

"Then Sarpene will become the true king and his power will be absolute. He will extend the Badlands over our whole world and nothing will be safe, not even the elves."

As the band stood, the only sound that could be heard was the swirling wind and waving leaves. The silence was finally broken by Midcraft.

"Can *you* defeat Sarpene?"

Tenii hesitated, and even the wind seemed to hesitate, waiting for an answer.

"I don't know." Tenii's eyes dropped. "But it is impossible without Dantin. Because he is the rightful heir, his presence within the castle should diminish Sarpene's power some."

"*Should,*" Narl scoffed. "We're supposed to put our necks on the line for what this half dwarf-half wizard says *should* happen?"

Tenii glared. Argo stepped forward.

"Regardless, we must fight."

Jumping up, Narl pressed his nose against Argo's.

"If a band of bloody gremlins can take us without a fight, how are we going to stand up to Sarpene?"

"Forget fighting Sarpene for now, Argo." Midcraft stepped in between the two elves. "Right now we have to go to the elves. Perhaps they will even help us."

This brought roaring laughter from the whole group.

"Elves helping us, that'll be the day."

"It's better than dying," Lentry added.

"Not much," Narl chuckled. "Byron, what of you, you haven't said a word."

The entire band quieted for the first time as Byron contemplated, looking each dwarf in the face in turn. After a moment of silence, he spoke softly.

"To go after Sarpene, we need all the help we can get. Whether it comes from elves, or the boy, we need help."

"What is a boy to do, he'll be bested within a few seconds of a fight," Narl argued.

"Not this boy," Tenii defended. "He'll make them think twice about fighting us."

"A boy?"

"Yes," Byron agreed. "There is something special about this boy, I saw it when the wolves were attacking him, and I can see it in his eyes when he talks. There is more to him than a simple boy."

"So what do you propose?" Lentry asked.

"We go after the boy and the fawn. If we can elicit the elves' help at the same time, then I will welcome it. If not, we make further plans when Dantin and Petra are with us."

"I will not die for a boy, even a prince. I've pledged no loyalty to the kingdom." Narl sat down as Margus and Avrom, two of his supporters, nervously looked around and sat on either side of him.

"Then so be it," Byron said dryly. "Stay here, and I will go after him, alone if I have to. But remember, it's true you've sworn no loyalty to the boy, but you have sworn it to me, and to your dwarven brothers."

To this, Narl had no response. He looked to the ground. Margus and Avrom stood again.

"I'll honor my loyalty to you Byron," Avrom stated, standing and lifting his arm. "I'll go where you go."

Byron nodded.

"And I too," Margus agreed, followed by pledges from the other dwarves present. Still, Narl said nothing.

"Then it is done. We leave now. Grab whatever food you can and as many weapons as you can carry. We'll nurse our headaches by beating up on some elves."

Tenii smiled and looked at Byron's solemn face. The dwarves cheered and raised their hands. Lentry placed a hand on Tenii's shoulder.

"Here we go, my friend."

Tenii raised his eyebrows and nodded a thanks.

Dantin lay stunned on the floor. His shoulder was scratched from the window frame and his hands felt as though they were about to fall off, but he was otherwise unhurt. He rolled over and inspected the room. It was a great deal bigger than the room he was kept in, but not nearly as well lit. A cabinet containing many strange-looking statues blocked out most of the sun, leaving many strange shadows upon the wall. Dantin pushed himself to his feet and went to the door, finding it locked just as securely as the one in his room. Discouraged, he leaned back against the door and ran his hands through his hair.

"Great, now what?" he said aloud, sliding down the door to his rear end. Out of the corner of his eye, he caught a slight movement in the shadows, making his heart skip a beat. He immediately slid the rest of the way onto his back and crawled into the opposite corner to hide in the shadow.

"Who's there?" he called, intentionally making his voice sound gruff and intimidating. The shape moved again, but did not answer. Dantin crept along the wall and got closer to the shadow it was hiding in. It shifted once more and Dantin was able to get a better look at its shape. It seemed to be no larger than himself, so taking a deep breath he lunged.

—BAM!

Missing the creature, Dantin slammed headfirst into the wall.

"Ohhhh," he groaned, rolling over and holding his head in his hands. He tried to open his eyes, but the room was spinning so fast it turned his stomach. Before he could figure out what happened, something was pushing onto his chest. He looked up again and saw the outline of a deer standing above him.

"What are you doing in here? They told me I'd be safe."

"Petra?" Dantin called in disbelief.

"Dantin?"

Petra pulled his hoof off of Dantin's chest and jumped down on top of him.

"Your Majesty, I can't believe it. I thought you'd be dead."

"Well, one more headfirst dive into the wall and I may be," Dantin replied, returning the fawn's affection and joy.

The two finished their joyful reunion and went to the door.

"How are we going to get out of here?" Dantin asked, pulling one more time on the knob.

"How did you get in here in the first place? You came crashing through the window like you could fly."

"They were keeping me in the room above this. I climbed down on a makeshift rope."

"Wow," Petra exclaimed. "You are creative. But now what?"

"I don't know." Dantin scratched his head and scanned the room for anything to use, but there was no rug, no table, nothing but the cabinet and the statues.

"Can we climb to the next room?" Dantin asked, going to the window.

"No, there's nothing but trees below." The next room down was twice as far as this one had been and Dantin could still see nothing but treetops below that.

Dantin scratched his head again.

"It won't be long before they discover that I'm gone, and with the rope still hanging out the window, they won't have to guess where I've gone." He let out a long sigh. "Our only chance is to rush whoever comes through this door. If they haven't been to my room yet, we can catch them by surprise."

As if what they were saying had been overheard, Petra and Dantin heard a door close and keys jingling on the other side of the door.

"Quick," Dantin whispered. "Back into the corner."

Petra scurried back to the corner and Dantin grabbed a statue from the cabinet and hid in the shadows by the door.

Hearing the lock pop and seeing the doorknob slowly turn, Dantin gripped his weapon and readied himself to spring. The door opened and a small elf entered carrying a plate of food in one hand and a ring of keys in the other. Dantin's eyes immediately fell on the large dagger the elf carried on his belt. He closed his eyes and prayed that he was alone.

"I have food for you," the elf called. He stopped and scanned the room for Petra. "Come out of there, deer, I'm not going to hurt you." He shook his head and took a step toward the corner Petra was hiding in.

—THUD!

Dantin crashed down upon the elf with the statue, sending the plate of food shattering to the floor and the elf laid out motionless. Dantin quickly looked outside the room for another guard, but found no one.

"Is he dead?" Petra asked squeamishly, coming out from his hiding place.

Dantin bent over and found the elf's pulse.

"No," he replied. "But his headache's going to be even worse than mine when he wakes up."

Petra let out a sigh of relief as Dantin picked up the keys and dagger.

"We have to hurry, they're probably bringing food to my room right now too."

The pair crept out of the room. A small window dimly lighted the hallway. They found an unlocked door at the end. Dantin gritted his teeth as he tried to open the door with as little noise as possible.

—CREAK.

The opening door seemed to echo endlessly both up and down a large stairway. Petra and Dantin both looked at each other, rolled their eyes and shook their heads at the same time. The dreary, torch-lit stairway spiraled down for what seemed like forever. Many of the landings led to doors the two didn't attempt. Dantin led the way with the dagger held up. The only sounds were Dantin's muffled footsteps and the clatter of Petra's hoofs.

"I guess we keep going down until it ends," Dantin whispered after many silent minutes.

"How do we know when we've reached the ground, what if the stairs keep on going?" Petra questioned hesitantly.

"Uh—I guess we just take our chances," Dantin answered almost humorously. "Then I guess we'll have to dig."

"Yeah," Petra answered rolling his eyes. "That's just what my hoofs were meant for."

They traveled uninterrupted for quite a while before they finally heard the noises they were dreading.

"Quick, the prisoners are missing," was a command accompanied by many soft footsteps scrambling up the stairs.

Dantin and Petra stopped dead in their tracks. There was no telling how far down the elves were, and the stairs left no chance to hide.

"Quick," Dantin whispered. "Back up to the next landing."

The footsteps got louder with every second. The two raced back up the stairs. As they ran, more and more sounds filled the stairwell as more elves joined the pursuit. They reached the landing and Dantin grabbed for the door.

"It's locked!" he whispered desperately.

"Of course it is," Petra answered. "Do you think they'd make this easy? Use the keys!"

"Wait," Dantin stopped suddenly. "There must be thirty keys here."

"They're right behind us, just try them."

Dantin fumbled the keys and tried a few with no luck.

"They all look exactly the same."

Key after key fit halfway into the lock but would not turn. Petra turned and looked down the stairway.

"Come on!" Dantin gritted through his teeth.

—CLANG!

The keys clattered to the floor and Dantin turned to Petra with a look of despair.

"It's not happening." Dantin took a deep breath and pulled the dagger back out. "Here, get behind me."

Dantin pushed Petra back into the corner and stood at the edge of the stairs, now hearing footfalls coming down the stairs as well.

"Whatever happens," Dantin called over his shoulder. "Stay behind—"

A hand gripped Dantin's shoulder and pulled him through the opened door. Dantin watched as the door closed the lighted stairway out, leaving him in complete darkness.

21

Unexpected Aid

"Petra!" Dantin called into the darkness, scrambling to his feet

"I'm here, Dantin," Petra answered, nudging his head into Dantin's side.

"How did you get the door opened?" Dantin laid his free hand on the fawn's head and raised the dagger into the darkness.

"I-I didn't."

A flash of light illuminated the room. Shielding his eyes, Dantin saw a hazy figure standing before him.

"Tierra," he cried in disbelief. "Wh-what are you—"

"Shhhh," Tierra hushed with a finger to her lips. The three stood silently, listening to the voices and footsteps grow louder, then slowly disappear. Tierra was the first to break the silence.

"What are you doing here?" she whispered.

"What are *we* doing here!?" Dantin answered in a harsh whisper. "What are *you* doing here?"

"I am a princess, thank you. I go where I please. Besides, these are *my* chambers."

Dantin's mouth dropped open as he looked around the room. The room sparkled, encased almost entirely in a snow white, silky valance. Just to his right stood a golden vanity full of hundreds of items Dantin couldn't begin to recognize and a stool covered completely with velvet. Petra couldn't pull his eyes off of the princess to admire the room.

"Why did you help us?" Dantin asked, returning his eyes to Tierra.

"I-I don't know." Tierra's eyes fell to the floor. "Where are you going?"

"Anywhere but here. We're not going to be prisoners—right, Petra? Petra?

Dantin turned to the fawn and snapped his fingers in front of his face.

"*Right*, Petra?"

"Uh—yeah, right." Petra shook his head and gave Dantin an embarrassed smile.

"Then take me with you," Tierra blurted.

Dantin was taken aback.

"Why would we take you with us?" Dantin asked

"They treat me like a child here. I can't go outside without guards, and even then I'm not allowed more than a couple hundred yards away. I want to see things, I want to—"

"Wait," Dantin interrupted. "I thought you were a princess and could go *anywhere* you wished."

The princess glared at Dantin's smirking face and dropped her hands to her hips.

"Well, are you going to take me or not?"

"No way! What need to we have for a snotty elf?"

"But Dantin, maybe—" Petra began.

"SNOTTY!" Tierra gasped. "I am ***not*** snotty. And I'll have you know that I'm an expert archer.

"So," Dantin answered, unimpressed.

"Fine." Tierra stood tall and walked toward the door. "I guess I'll just have to call the guards."

"Dantin?" Petra pleaded.

Dantin watched her go the door and begin to turn the knob.

"FINE!" Dantin called, throwing his hands in the air.

Tierra turned, smiling bigger than an angel.

"Great."

Dantin shook his head and gave Petra a dirty look for now carrying the smirk. Tierra went to her closet and disappeared, returning a moment later, transformed from an innocent-looking elfin princess to a warrior, complete with chain-link vest, helmet, bow, and quiver full of arrows.

"Let's go," she beamed.

Both Dantin and Petra's mouths dropped to the floor at the transformation.

"You're forgetting, Princess," Dantin said, regaining his composure, "the guards are all over this place looking for us. We're not just going to waltz out the door and down the steps."

"Of course not, I know a better way."

Tierra went to the side of her bed, pushed a table out of the way, lifted a rug, and pulled a trap door.

"Not many of the elves here know of this passage." With another smile, she threw her bow over her shoulder and disappeared into the floor.

"Tell me again why you didn't want her coming with us," Petra taunted with his smirk returning.

"Oh, shut up," Dantin responded, climbing through the door.

Petra laughed and followed.

Once they were all in, Tierra turned and pulled a rope that closed and re-covered the door with the rug.

The path they traveled was narrow and dimly lit by a torch Tierra carried.

"What's that smell?" Petra complained. "It's worse than Dantin's feet."

"Hey." Dantin turned and shot Petra another dirty look.

"These passages haven't been used for hundreds of years, and even then they were only used to transport prisoners and make deliveries throughout the castle. Oh, and Dantin, I have a potion that can take care of that foot odor problem," Tierra teased.

"That's quite all right," Dantin replied, shooting Petra another look as the fawn burst into laughter.

The three traveled a while longer in silence before they came to an open room with low ceilings. There were two doorways on either side of the room and a trap door in the ceiling. Petra looked back at the wall behind him as the shadows danced upon the wall.

"We're just below the throne room," Tierra said, pointing to the trap door.

"How did you find all this?" Dantin asked, trying not to sound impressed.

"When they don't let you explore outside, you have to find other things to explore. I found the door in my room a couple years ago, and I've been coming down here to get away ever since. If you stand close enough to the door in the ceiling, you can hear the meetings they hold in the throne room."

"So that's how you found me," Dantin realized.

Tierra blushed and shrugged.

"That hallway will lead us to the forest."

"What are we waiting for," Petra said excitedly. "Let's go."

"SHHH, wait." Tierra pointed again to the trap door as they heard the clatter of footsteps above them. They moved closer to hear what was going on above them.

"Your Majesty," a gruff voice announced. "The prisoners are gone. Their rooms are empty and we found an unconscious elf in the fawn's room and his keys were not with him."

"That's Harrod, the captain of the guards," Tierra whispered.

"Did you search the castle?"

"That's my mother," she followed.

"Yeah, I figured, now be quiet," Dantin commanded.

"We're searching now," Harrod answered.

"Keep searching," the queen demanded. "We cannot let that boy go anywhere where Sarpene can get him."

"Well," the elf hesitated. "We found the guard's keys in one of the stairways, but—"

"But what? What are you trying to tell me?"

"Well, Your Majesty, we found the guard's keys—"

"Where?" The queen could feel the tension in the elf's voice.

"Outside Tierra's chambers, and she is not in there."

"They took my little girl?" Queen Sylvania gasped.

"I-I don't think so. We searched the room and found no sign of a struggle, and her mail, helmet, and bow are all missing."

"What are you saying? You think she's with them willingly?"

"It looks like she's helping them, Your Highness."

"Then don't waste your time here talking to me. Search every inch of this castle, and place guards on every door leading to the forest."

"We've already placed the guards, but we are still searching."

"Good, now go find my little girl."

"Yes, ma'am." They heard the guard turn and run from the room, leaving the queen alone. After a few seconds they could hear faint sobs from above.

Dantin's heart sank.

"Maybe you should stay here," he offered. "She seems to care a great deal for you."

"Of course she cares for me, she's my mother. Doesn't your mother—oh, yeah."

Tierra bit her lip as Dantin's eyes sank to the floor. Petra nuzzled his nose into Dantin's side.

"Besides," Tierra started, trying to break the moment. "I'm already in trouble, what's a little more trouble going to get me?"

"Well, you don't know us very well," Petra chuckled. "We find trouble every time we turn around."

"Are you sure you want to go with us?" Dantin asked, trying not to sound like he was trying to talk her into it.

"Of course, I need an adventure. Let's go."

Tierra took off in the direction of the hallway she had pointed to earlier.

"Wait," Petra called. "I thought you said this door led to the dungeons and the other led to the forest."

"You heard my mother, they're guarding all the doors leading to the forest."

Petra looked to Dantin.

"Then what are we going to do?"

"There's a garbage shoot in the dungeons that leads outside. I doubt they'll be watching that."

"Let's hope not," Dantin sighed as Tierra vanished through the door. He turned and raised his eyebrows to Petra and they both followed. The path twisted and turned, and they seemed to be traveling steadily downward as they walked in relative silence. Every once in a while either Petra or Dantin would stumble over something or run into a wall, following with a couple quiet curses and mumbling. Dantin was amazed at how well Tierra moved through the tunnel. She had seemed like a prissy girl who was afraid to get her dress dirty, but now she was moving through the dark, damp spaces like a sewer rat, fluidly dodging obstacles as if she'd traveled this road thousands of times.

As they walked, Dantin silently wondered why he had really let her come with them, and even why she wanted to. They could have made it from the throne room without any help. Why was she getting herself into even more trouble and even putting herself in danger to help them? Besides, once they reached the forest, what good was she going to be then? She had said herself that she'd never ventured into the forest more than a couple hundred yards. She couldn't be their guide and she couldn't fight off wolves (no girl could). She was probably just going to slow them down and whine about her feet hurting or something.

But still, as they walked, Dantin kept looking up at her in amazement. The torch left a golden halo around her body that sparkled off her mail. She almost looked like a couple of those Greek goddesses he'd studied in school. Athena, he remembered, the goddess of war, clad fully in body armor carrying a fierce, yet beautiful smile. And who was the other goddess she reminded him of? Dantin racked his brain, trying to come up with the name. He remembered the pictures of her from his mythology book. He could picture her in his mind, dressed in silky white gowns with her angle-like face and rosy cheeks, sitting upon a large clamshell. Dantin pleaded with himself to remember her name, it was on the tip of his tongue, but he couldn't quite spit it out. Aphrodite! That was it, Aphrodite. He finally got it. He smiled to himself for remembering. Aphrodite, the goddess of lov— He stopped suddenly.

"Dantin," he gritted through his teeth aloud. *"She's a girl."*

"What's that, Dantin?" Tierra asked, turning and looking.

Dantin chuckled nervously, silently grateful the dark would not give away his blushing face.

"Uh—nothing. I-I thought I saw a birl."

"A what?" she asked, confused.

"Y-you know, a-a birl. It's a thing where I come from."

Tierra rolled her eyes and turned back around.

"Okay, whatever," she said.

Dantin slapped his forehead. What the heck is a *birl*? He shook his head and continued.

"Great going, Dantin," Petra teased in a whisper. "You're real smooth with the ladies, aren't you."

"Shut up," he gritted through his teeth.

"We're almost there." Tierra turned, pretending she couldn't hear their conversation.

Dantin grunted his approval and shot a look to Petra pleading with him to be quiet. Petra smiled, over exaggerating closing his mouth. Dantin chuckled and turned forward again, noticing the tunnel changing. Their path narrowed and the ceiling lowered as they walked.

"How much smaller does this get?" Dantin asked, having to hunch so as not to bump his head.

"It gets to be a tight squeeze, but it's manageable," Tierra returned, turning sideways and shuffling against the narrow walls.

"I hope you're not claustrophobic, Petra," Dantin teased.

"Claustra-what-ic?" Petra asked.

"Claustro-*pho*-bic, it means afraid of small spaces."

"I'm not afraid of anything," Petra beamed, puffing out his chest, but suddenly noticing how close the walls were getting.

"Oh yeah, that's right," Dantin patronized. "That except for wolves, right?"

"Yeah, wolves." Petra shuddered.

"And spiders too, right."

"Spiders too," Petra sighed.

"What about heights, and the dark, and the *boogeyman*?"

"What's the boogeyman?" Petra asked, gulping.

"He's a monster that hides under beds and in closets. He only comes out late at night when you're alone in a room." Dantin looked back and saw Petra's eyes grow twice their normal size.

"N-naw, I'm not afraid of that."

"What about you, Tierra, are you afraid of the *boogeyman*?" he grumbled, letting off a sinister laugh.

"Would you two stop with that macho garbage," she responded, hiding a shudder at the thought of being attacked while she slept.

"Hey," Dantin laughed. "I'm just trying to warn you guys. The boogeyman's big back where I come from. All the kids have stories about him."

"Well, I don't want to hear it. Now be quiet, the dungeons are right around this bend."

Dantin chuckled, but didn't respond. Almost crawling through the small space, they rounded the bend, coming to a ledge.

"Be careful with the ledge, it's a little tricky," Tierra warned.

She positioned herself and jumped down with a small thud. Dantin reached the edge and looked down, seeing a drop of about five feet. He rolled his eyes.

"Careful? For this small jump?" he boasted. I used to jump out of trees twice as—"

—THUD!

Dantin's foot caught the edge as he tried to twist, sending him slamming straight on his back.

"See," he winced, scrambling to his feet and trying not to lose his breath. "I told you there's no problem."

"I am impressed," Tierra tried to hide her laughter as Petra's head poked through the opening.

"What happened?"

"Dantin was showing off his acrobatics," Tierra laughed.

"Never mind," Dantin grumbled. "Just get down here."

Petra squeezed forward, and jumped, gracefully landing on all fours.

"Now that was impressive, Dantin."

"Whatever. Where is this garbage chute?

Tierra and Petra exchanged smiling glances and Tierra pointed to a trap door in the floor.

"Down through there is the dungeons. The chute is in there."

"Won't there be guards in the dungeons?" Petra asked hesitantly.

"Not if they're all out looking for me. See, I told you I'd get you out of here."

Tierra and Dantin grasped at the handle at the same time, bumping hands.

"Oh, I-I was just—" Dantin stuttered.

"N-no, go ahead," Tierra directed, equally as flustered.

Dantin pulled the door up with a loud creak, wincing at the noise.

"Well, if there are any guards in there, they know we're coming."

Dantin grabbed the torch from Tierra and stuck his head through the hole. There were a few empty cells right below them and a long hallway. He listened and could hear a strange whining noise coming from the dark hallway. Hoping it was just the door still echoing, he jumped down, this time landing on his feet. He shook his head and wondered if they had seen that jump. Looking around, the room looked creepier from the ground. The flickering torch left strange shadows on everything, and even hid a few corners. A chilled breeze hit him, sending shivers up and down his spine. He shook them away and put the torch in a holder that looked like a large dragon's head.

"It's clear," he called up. "Come on down."

Tierra was the first to jump down. Dantin tried to reach out and catch her, but they both went tumbling to the floor. With wide eyes, he rushed to his feet and tried to help Tierra to hers.

"I'm fine, help Petra."

Petra jumped through and landed on all fours again.

"Over there." Tierra pointed.

Dantin saw a square metal cover with a small handle. He pulled it out, and it creaked louder than the trap door had.

"Now what?" he asked.

"Now we go for a ride. Who's first?"

"I want to go first this time," Petra chimed.

"Alright, buddy, let's go." Dantin held out his hands for Petra to step into.

"Ugh, how much can you weigh?" he gritted.

"Too many bugs, huh?" Petra snorted. He got his head through and slid away.

"Here, you go next," Dantin offered timidly.

Hoisting the princess up, Dantin watched her position herself and slide into the darkness. When the sound of her sliding faded away, he pulled himself up and followed, wondering what to expect on the outside.

22

Caught

"Something's not right," Byron exclaimed, jumping from a low-hanging tree branch.

"What do you mean, what has to be right for us to attack?" Argo questioned, pulling his axe from his belt.

"The squirrels tell me they have multiple guards at every entrance to the castle, and search parties throughout the area."

"Do they know we're coming?"

Byron scratched his beard.

"I don't think so, they wouldn't have let us get this far if they had. Their search efforts seem to be from the castle out."

"Then let's take the search parties one by one, then go after the entrances."

"Patience, Argo, we cannot attack until we know what's going on."

Tenii stepped forward.

"Let me sneak forward and get a better look at what's happening. I can disguise myself and blend in."

"Why you?" Avrom complained. "Why not send me? I'm much better in the woods."

"No," Byron shook his head. "I'll go with Tenii."

"Then I'm coming too," Argo asserted. "I'm not staying here while you guys have all the fun."

"I'm with Argo," Lentry followed, raising his axe.

"And I too," Midcraft added. "I'm not letting you go near there without me, big brother. You're getting old, someone has to watch your back."

The whole band laughed and Byron smiled.

"Thank you, brother, for the vote of confidence, but I think my old bones still have some sneaking around in them. Besides, too many of us will draw too much attention. I promise, we won't have any fun without you."

Tenii reached into his pouch and pulled out a small flask filled with powder.

"This will camouflage us. It's not perfect, but we won't be seen unless they look directly at us."

Byron nodded as Tenii sprinkled the powder on his head.

"*Incantatious dominos incompareo,*" Tenii chanted.

"Whoa, I guess you're more wizard than I thought," Lentry exclaimed as the image of his brother faded. As Tenii said, they could still see him when they looked directly, but out of the corner of their eyes, he looked a bush.

"Thank you, my friend," Tenii blushed and repeated the process on himself.

"Remember," Byron commanded as Tenii disappeared, "stay out of sight, and don't start anything."

"Why are you looking at me?" Argo defended. "You are looking at me, aren't you?"

"Of course he is," Midcraft laughed and patted Argo's shoulder. "Who else would start a fight in a strange land when we're outnumbered a hundred to one?"

Argo shrugged his shoulders in agreement and smiled.

"We could take them."

Disappearing into the brush, Byron turned and addressed the band again.

"If we're not back by nightfall, go back to the caves and regroup there. Do *not* come after us!"

"Yeah, sure, whatever," Lentry agreed, rolling his eyes. "We'll let them keep you forever."

Byron turned without response and within seconds, they were gone, only being given away by an occasional shaking of a bush or swaying of a tree limb.

As they crept along, Tenii noticed for the first time the sweetness of the air they were breathing. With all of their traveling through the badlands, and even in Kudosh, Tenii didn't realize how much he missed fresh air and cool breezes. He immediately missed his home and the wide fields filled with flowers and the gentle brook. He shook the thoughts from his head and remembered his task. Following Byron close, he ducked behind bushes and slid behind trees when they were close enough. The two made slow time, but they were almost silent, except for the occasional breaking twig and the clatter of Dantin's sword hanging from his hip.

"Wow," Tenii exclaimed as the castle came into view. It almost looked like a large cluster of trees, with the middle one towering high above the others, getting lost in the clouds above. They stopped and scanned the area, spotting the entrances guarded by elves.

"There's four or five elves at every entrance," Byron whispered. "I haven't seen any of the search parties though."

"Do you know of any secret entrances?" Tenii asked.

Byron shook his head.

"Where do we go now?"

"Let's go around to the back. Maybe there is a weakness there."

Tenii nodded and the two continued in silence, keeping a constant eye out for the search parties. After half an hour, Tenii looked up and could still see part of the front of the castle.

"Geez, how big is this thing?"

"This is the first time I've been here. I've heard hundreds of stories, but none of them did justice to how massive it is."

After another hour, the reached a spot where they could stop again.

"I don't see any more guards," Tenii observed.

"No, but I don't see any entrances either." Byron looked toward the sky. "It's growing dark. We need to make our way back and regroup.

"Alright, but—"

—Crash!

A boot to the head sprawled Tenii to the ground, taking Byron with him. As he turned over, he saw two elves standing over them, bows bent and arrows aimed at their heads.

"You dwarves smell of Kudosh and wolves," the elf proclaimed.

"Great vanishing spell," Byron grumbled.

"Hey, who knew we smelled?" Tenii defended.

"You're intruding in the queen's land," the elf continued. "By all rights, we could kill you now."

Tenii closed his eyes.

"Let go of that bow, and say goodbye to your head." The familiar voice came from behind the elves. Tenii opened his eyes and saw Argo holding his axe ready to strike.

"Argo," Byron yelled. "What are you doing here?"

"Saving your skin, that's what. I told you not to have any fun without me."

The elves relaxed their bows and looked at each other.

"What do you say we take some elf heads," Argo winked.

"You're not that fast, dwarf." Argo turned his head and saw another elf behind him, with an arrow aimed toward his back.

"Look around," the elf commanded.

Argo looked up and saw they were surrounded by at least ten elves, each with bows flexed.

"You didn't happen to bring the others, did you, Argo?" Tenii asked with wide eyes.

"Sorry," Argo shrugged, dropping the axe.

"Should we kill them, Harrod?" one elf asked.

"WAIT!" Byron shouted, sitting up. "We have no wish to fight. We are looking for two lost companions and were seeking your help."

"We know nothing of lost companions," an elf barked, kicking Byron back to the ground. "You're trespassing!"

"You are Harrod?" Tenii interrupted.

The elf nodded.

"We met once, long ago. You came and negotiated for your queen with my master, King Fintabi. I am Tenii, his loyal servant."

"Yes, I remember you. Fintabi is no longer in power, why are you in my queen's land?"

"As we said, we are searching for lost companions. One is the son of King Fintabi, Prince Dantin."

"Once again," Harrod slowly gritted through his teeth. "We know nothing of lost companions and I am losing patience."

"Take us to your queen and we will explain everything."

Harrod walked over and talked with another elf. He returned a moment later.

"Where are the others you mentioned?"

"Far away," Argo broke in. "They grew impatient and returned to the cave."

Harrod thought for a minute, then replaced his arrow in his quiver and his bow upon his shoulder.

"If the queen will see you, so be it. But if not, we have nice places in the dungeon for you."

"Fair enough," Tenii conceded.

"Shackle them, and take their weapons," Harrod commanded. Then he hesitated as he looked intently at the sword Tenii was carrying for Dantin. He shot a questioning glance at Tenii, then looked back to the sword. Without response, he took it up and carried it himself.

The dwarves were brought to their feet and shackles were placed around their wrists and ankles.

"I hope this works," Byron whispered to Tenii.

"So do I," Tenii responded, closing his eyes and praying again.

23

Waste Deep

"EWWW, what is this stuff?" Dantin lifted his hand and a thick green slime oozed through his fingers.

"You don't want to know," Tierra laughed, reaching out and helping him up.

"What's that smell?" Dantin crinkled his nose and his eyes began to water.

"You don't want to know that either. Here, we can get out over there." She pointed to a low edge of the garbage bin. They trudged over, knee deep in the nastiest brown goop Dantin had ever seen or smelled, and found Petra hanging his head over the edge.

"You all right, buddy?"

Petra pulled back over the edge with his eyes watering and a painful look on his face.

"It's funny," he sputtered. "I haven't eaten anything, but I definitely have something in my stomach to lose. I-I've never—"

"Wow, I didn't know deer could turn green," Dantin laughed as Petra's head went back over the edge. "This kinda reminds me of my room one week when Ms. Mullin was on vacation. What is this stuff?"

"All the castle's waste ends up here. When it rots, they spread it over the fields."

"Oh, that's a pretty good idea—" Dantin started, interrupting himself with another thought. "Wait. When you say all the castle's waste, you don't mean—"

"*All* the waste comes here," she said with a knowing look. "We probably don't want to spend too much time in here."

It was Dantin's turn to turn green and lose everything in his almost empty stomach. Tierra rolled her eyes at both of them and looked over the edge for guards.

"It's clear. When you guys are finished, we have to get out of here."

Dantin looked at her with his eyes half closed and his stomach doing somersaults.

"Wow, that's cute," Tierra laughed, pointing to the line of slobber hanging from Dantin's lip to the ground. Dantin quickly found a clean spot on his shirt and wiped his face, trying desperately to regain his composure. Tierra laughed again and climbed over the edge. Dantin and Petra looked at each other and dove over the edge together, sprawling on the ground and rolling around.

"That's soooo gross," Dantin complained, rolling around in the grass as he tried to get everything off of himself. Petra did the same until Tierra finally stopped them.

"Would you two babies stop it? We've got to go hide." She looked up toward the sky. "The sun's almost down. There's a thicket back here we can hide in until nightfall."

Tierra scanned the area again and took off toward the forest. Dantin scrambled to his feet and followed, with Petra right on his heels. As they were running Dantin seemed to hit every hanging branch and bush along the way.

"Isn't there some kind of path we could be—?"

—Whack!

"Geez, could you watch it, you're going to put my eye out," Dantin yelled, pushing the bent branch that just whacked him in the face to the side.

"Quiet, we're almost there," she called back.

Dantin grunted and continued. After a few more minutes, Dantin saw Tierra disappear into a clump of bushes. He followed through and found himself in a clearing no bigger than the closet he used to sleep in. A couple seconds later Petra was through.

"This isn't bad," Dantin exclaimed, seeing that they were completely surrounded by large trees and thick bushes. "Nobody can see into here."

"I know. I used to come here and hide when I'd get into a fight with my mother. They could never find me," she said with a wry smile. "We'll be safe here until dark, it should only be a couple hours."

"Great, I could use some rest," Petra proclaimed, immediately lying down. Dantin and Tierra smiled to each other as they saw the fawn fall asleep in only a few seconds.

"Yeah, I guess I could use some rest too," Dantin yawned, sitting down and leaning back against a tree. Tierra did the same, as far away from Dantin as possible, of course.

As they both closed their eyes, Dantin began to wonder aloud.

"So where is your father?" he asked innocently. "I've met your mother, and everybody mentions the 'queen's land' and stuff like that, but nobody has mentioned a king."

Tierra was silent, and Dantin thought she'd fallen asleep as fast as Petra, but her silence was broken by a sigh a moment later.

"A long time ago, longer ago than I can even remember, my father led a band of elves against Sarpene. He was a great friend of your father's and they wanted to free him."

"What happened?" Dantin sat back up and opened his eyes.

Tierra hesitated and sighed.

"My mother told me that a couple of weeks later, about half of the elves my father took with him returned, beaten and battered, many near death. They told my mother that my father refused to leave the injured and slain elves behind, so he continued fighting until he was killed as well." Two large tears rolled down Tierra's cheek from her closed eyes.

"I-I'm sorry. I didn't know."

"It's okay, it's something I've grown to deal with. But not a day has gone by that I haven't hated Sarpene for taking my father from me."

"I know the feeling." Dantin leaned back, trying to keep tears of his own from building up.

"My mother tells me all the time how much I'm like him, strong, but stubborn. She knows that I'd go after Sarpene myself if I could. That's why I always have a guard with me. It's not to protect me, it's to keep me from going after him."

"So that's why you wanted to come with us, to go after Sarpene?" Dantin sat up again and looked toward Tierra, but her eyes remained closed and the tears dried.

"They keep telling me that revenge is a horrible thing, but I've thought about it every day for eleven years now. All I need is one shot, I can hit a small apple from seventy paces." She nodded to herself. "I could put one in his chest if I had the chance."

"Well," Dantin sighed and lay back for the last time. "Maybe we can avenge your father and save mine at the same time."

Tierra finally looked up and smiled.

"Thanks," she said, but Dantin was already asleep.

24

Alliance

The elves led Tenii, Byron, and Argo down a long, dark hallway

"Hey, watch it!" Argo barked as he was shoved in the shoulder.

"Quiet, dwarf," the elf responded, shoving him again.

"Calm down, Argo," Byron urged. "Don't make it worse than it already is."

"Then tell this gremlin to quit pushing me."

"Gremlin, huh?" the elf laughed. "This *gremlin* could have killed you a few minutes ago."

Argo stopped cold and turned to the guard.

"Then take these shackles off and we can have a go at it," he spat.

"Oh, you'd like that, wouldn't you," the elf laughed again, pushing Argo even harder. "Now get back in line, or we might have to."

"Sumptus," Harrod called from the front of the line. "Leave the dwarf alone and go back to your post."

"We'll discuss this later," Argo glared and started walking again.

"You can bet on it, I'll—"

"SUMPTUS!"

"Yes, sir, right away." The elf turned and ran away while Argo smirked.

Harrod led them past doorway after doorway, until they reached two great, red doors. The intricate carvings covering them carried symbols of the elf kingdom and many symbols of nature. Tenii also noticed King Fintabi's seal, a kingly figure seated upon clouds holding a scepter in one hand and a dove in the other, surrounded by a giant sun in the background, etched into the wood. The golden handles of the door were also in the shape of doves, flying from tree branches.

"Wait here," Harrod commanded, and entered the room. The three dwarves stood among the five remaining guards and Argo assessed the situation.

"We can take these guys," he whispered to Byron.

"Argo," Byron warned. "We have no weapons, we are shackled, and we are in a castle that none of us are familiar with. Don't even think about it."

"But I could take these guys alo—"

"No!"

"Quiet," one of the guards commanded.

Argo rolled his eyes and cursed under his breath.

After a few moments, the doors opened again and Harrod emerged.

"The queen will see you," he said reluctantly.

Before they entered, Byron turned to Argo.

"When we talk to the queen, do not say a word. Tenii and I will take care of it. We don't need you causing trouble."

"What kind of trouble could I cause?" Argo asked innocently.

"We have an objective, and ill-placed comments could ruin it all. Just keep your mouth shut." Argo could see from Byron's eyes that he was serious.

"Fine," he conceded.

The three dwarves were herded through the door and into a room larger than Tenii had ever seen. They walked upon a soft red carpet through many rows of statues of elves and beautiful fairies upon fountains. Tenii stared in awe upon the stunning artwork that covered every wall from floor to ceiling, depicting famous battles in history and great rulers throughout the years. Tenii even saw a painting of King Tanupa, his wife and Fintabi as a child. Glass windows in the ceiling let him know the sun had already set, yet the room seemed to be brighter than any sunny day he'd ever experienced. As they approached the throne, the queen, dressed in a pure white satin dress and golden headdress, stood and motioned to the guards on either side of her to stay. She stepped down three steps and awaited the dwarves.

"Here are our prisoners, Your Majesty," Harrod announced with a bow, then stood aside. The queen looked at each of them intently. It was a long moment before she spoke.

"Tenii," she began. "It has been a long time, my old friend. It's too bad it could not be under happier circumstances."

"Yes, it has, Your Majesty," Tenii said, bowing as much as his chains would allow. "And I wish this visit was under better circumstances as well."

The queen acknowledged his bow and turned to Byron.

"And you are Byron, I presume."

The dwarf nodded, but did not bow.

"I have heard a lot of stories about you, you seem to be a great warrior."

Byron nodded again, but did not respond.

"What right do you have attacking my castle? Great warrior or not, you don't stand a chance."

"We did not attack your castle, Your Majesty," Byron finally spoke. "We are simply searching for lost companions, and have reason to believe they are in this area."

The queen nodded, and approached Argo, gently stroking his bearded face.

"Who might this be, and why does he hold such contempt for me in his eyes?"

Argo began to respond, but Tenii cut him off.

"This is Argo, another of our companions," he said, staring Argo down, begging him to keep quiet. "Forgive him, Your Majesty, for he is not as cultured in your traditions as I."

The queen nodded again and smiled, pulling her hand away before Argo could bite a finger off. Walking back to her throne, she began again.

"So tell me again why you are trespassing in my kingdom, armed for a battle. And where did you get this sword?" she asked, producing the Gladius Aspectus.

"Begging you pardon," Byron answered. "But two days ago our home was attacked and two of our companions were kidnapped. After the attack, we found elfin arrows that carried your mark. We came to get them back, and did not know what to expect, so yes, we armed heavily."

"And the sword?"

"It belongs to one of our kidnapped companions."

"But you were planning to attack my castle?" she asked, raising her eyebrows.

Bowing again, Tenii answered.

"We were here first to negotiate their return. They are dear companions and important to our quest."

"And if negotiations failed?"

"Then yes, we would have attacked."

"I see," she said, rising again. "These companions must be dear to attempt such a foolish move."

"I am sworn to protect one of the companions, giving my own life if necessary," Tenii responded.

The queen was silent again, contemplating what to say next.

"What if I were to tell you," she began after some time. "That I do not have you companions?"

"I would strongly urge you to reconsider, Your Majesty," Byron responded.

"Your Majesty," Tenii broke in before she could respond. "I noticed the seal of the Pangadesh kingdom on your door, and I see the painting of the king on your wall."

The queen nodded.

"Well, one of the companions is Dantin, son of King Fintabi."

"And," the queen followed.

"Your Majesty, with all due respect, Sarpene cannot stay in power forever. When Fintabi regains the throne, I assure you he will not be pleased to learn that you did not do all within you power to aid in the safety and protection of his son."

"How dare you threaten the queen," Harrod barked, raising his hand to slap Tenii.

"No, Harrod," the queen said calmly. "Tenii is right, Fintabi would not be happy if I did not protect his son." She looked more closely at Tenii. "Nor would he be happy to hear that his servant has placed his son's life in danger by attacking Sarpene with nothing but a misfit band of dwarves and a young boy."

"That is a matter between Fintabi and Tenii," Byron broke in. "Our only concern is to get the boy and the fawn back."

The queen went silent once again, pacing back and forth.

"As I said, I do not have your friends."

Tenii lowered his head and Byron's eyes closed to slits and grew red.

"They were here, under my *protection.* But they escaped, and took my daughter with them. It seems the boy is as resourceful as his father."

"That he is," Tenii smiled. "When did they escape?"

"Earlier today."

"Then why are we going through all of this if you already knew what was going on?" Argo barked, unable to contain himself anymore.

"We had to make sure you didn't have my daughter and were demanding ransom."

"So now what?" Tenii asked.

"Now we wait unti—"

Another elf came flying into the room.

"Y-Your Majesty," he exclaimed breathlessly. "We're under attack."

"What?" Harrod jumped to attention. "By who?"

"More dwarves, sir."

Harrod jumped down and grabbed Argo's shackles.

"You told me the others turned back," he barked.

"Yeah, well you told me you knew nothing about our friends. And besides, what kind of captain believes what his prisoners say?"

Harrod pulled back to strike Argo, but Byron intervened.

"Your Majesty, I can end this attack. They're coming to rescue us. I can stop them."

"We can handle a band of dwarves," Harrod proclaimed, forgetting Argo.

"Your Majesty, no elves *or* dwarves need to die over this. Let me loose and I'll stop them," Byron pleaded.

"But Your Majesty, I can—"

"Release him," she commanded.

Harrod roughly grabbed Byron's shackles and released him.

"Which way?" Byron asked, rubbing his wrists.

"Come on," Harrod said reluctantly. "Follow me."

They raced down the long hallway Byron had just been brought up in chains. When they reached the end, Harrod took a quick left and they ran down an equally long hallway, lighted with torches and decorated with more paintings and statues. At the end stood two enormous green doors. Harrod stopped at the doors and turned to Byron.

"Now what?" he asked.

"You stop your elves, and I'll go after my dwarves."

"How do I know I can trust you?"

Byron looked at the elf, winked, and smiled.

"I guess you can't know for sure." With that, he pulled the door open and disappeared into a thicket of bushes. Dodging a flurry of arrows, Byron bounced from tree to tree, shielding himself from the castle.

"Midcraft, Lentry," he yelled, but got no response. He continued zigzagging throughout the bushes until he spotted a bush moving violently.

"STOP!" he screamed, bursting through the bush and finding Marcum fighting with an elf. The dwarf threw the elf to the ground and raised his axe.

"Goodbye, gremlin," he called, bringing the axe down with full force.

"NO!" Byron dove in and tackled the dwarf before the axe hit its mark.

The elf scrambled to his feet and took off through the bushes.

"Byron?" Marcum shouted in disbelief. "What are you doing? You let him go!"

"We are at peace, my friend, there is no need to fight."

An arrow plunged into the ground inches from the two dwarves.

"What kind of peace is this?" Marcum scoffed, pulling himself to his feet.

"I'll explain later. Where are the others?"

The dwarf turned and pointed.

"Lentry is leading a few up the middle, and Midcraft has the rest further on, trying to flank them."

"You're alone here?"

"No, Avrom was with me, but that gremlin you let get away shot him."

Byron's eyes widened with horror.

"Is he—" he began, trailing off.

"No, he was hit in the shoulder."

Byron sighed and shook his head.

"Tend to him, I'll go after the others."

Taking off in the direction Marcum pointed, Byron noticed the flurry of arrows from the castle slow. He jumped a bush and found Lentry and an elf wrestling on the ground, each with a blade to the other's throat.

"STOP, it's over," he yelled, pulling the two apart. The elf rolled off smoothly and was back on his feet, holding the blade to Byron.

"You little—" Lentry growled approaching the two.

"Lentry, no, it's over."

The elf looked back and forth from dwarf to dwarf with scared eyes.

"I've spoken to your queen," Byron urged the elf. "It's over, we are at peace."

The elf didn't respond and kept the blade up, moving it from Lentry to Byron.

"See," he pointed. "Your friends in the castle aren't shooting any more arrows."

The elf turned his head for a second and Byron lunged, knocking the blade from his hands. Pinning the elf to the ground, he spoke again.

"I tell you we are at peace."

"Why should I believe you?" the elf spat.

"Because I'm letting you go and not cutting your throat." Byron rolled off the elf and stood. "Lentry, go make sure the others are okay."

Lentry nodded and took off. As soon as Byron was off the elf, he, too, took off toward the castle.

Within a few minutes, all the dwarves had been gathered and they found Byron resting against a tree. Marcum approached, supporting Avrom as he stumbled along with an arrow sticking from his left shoulder.

Midcraft looked at the pair and laughed.

"Not quite quick enough, huh Avrom?"

"It was a lucky shot," Avrom winced. "He's lucky he didn't lose his head."

All of the dwarves gathered questioningly around Byron.

"Where are Argo and Tenii?" one asked.

"They are safe in the castle."

"And the boy and fawn?"

Byron stood and smiled.

"They escaped before we got here. I guess there really *is* more to that boy than we thought," he commented with an impressed smile. Then he addressed Lentry.

"What happened, I thought I told you not to come after me?"

"Well," Lentry began. "A few minutes after you left, Argo disappeared, and you didn't say anything about not going after him."

Byron smiled and rubbed his scruffy beard, picking leaves and twigs from it.

"So what do we do now?" Midcraft asked.

"Set up camp here. I have to go talk to the queen again," Byron said. "Come, Avrom, we'll have that looked at."

"I'm not letting those nasty gremlins touch me," he scoffed, trying to stand up straight, but falling back upon Marcum's shoulders.

"Their healing methods are much better than yours or mine, my friend. Come." He motioned and Avrom reluctantly took hold of his shoulder and let him lead him to the castle.

"Don't start any more trouble, guys," he called over his shoulder.

"We'll be fine, Father," Midcraft called back, bringing laughter from the whole group.

Shaking his head, Byron led Avrom away, finding Harrod and a few guards on the steps of the castle awaiting them.

"Is he hurt badly?" Harrod asked.

"He'll live, but it needs attention," Byron grunted, pushing Avrom's dead weight up the stairs.

Harrod turned to one of the elves.

"Take him to Medeor, he'll have herbs to heal the wound."

Two elves approached Avrom and took either arm, but he shooed them off.

"I can walk," he grumbled, but after one step, he fell to his knees.

"He's a bit stubborn," Byron stated. "Let them help you, Avrom, I'm sure they have some whiskey to help with the pain."

At those words, Avrom brightened and placed his arms around the elves.

"Why didn't you tell me that before? Let's go," he instructed the elves.

"Dwarves are very interesting creatures," Harrod said as he watched the trio stumble down the hallway with Avrom cursing every three steps.

"That we are," Byron answered. "Almost as interesting as elves."

The two captains looked at each other and exchanged nods of respect for the first time.

"I must speak to the queen again," Byron said.

Harrod nodded and led Byron through the door again. As they entered, they found Argo wandering around.

"How do you get out of this cursed place?" Argo complained. "Is the battle over already?"

"Sorry, my friend," Byron said. "But I guess I had all the fun without you again."

Argo grumbled and stomped the floor.

"Where are the others?"

"Just outside, they'll be excited to hear our story."

Brightening, Argo burst through the door and out of sight.

"Very interesting," Harrod repeated with a sigh, tuning down the hallway.

The two reached the throne room again and entered without announcement, finding Tenii and the queen deep in conversation.

"Excuse the interruption, Your Majesty," Harrod bowed. "But the attack has been stopped and the dwarves have set up camp just outside the castle."

"Fine," she nodded to Harrod, then turned to a guard standing above her. "Send food to the camp, but keep guards close by to prevent any more altercations."

"Yes, ma'am," the elf responded and turned and walked away.

"Thank you, Your Majesty," Byron said, bowing to her for the first time.

The queen nodded and began again.

"Tenii has been explaining your quest to me. It seems as though the boy has already been through quite a bit. He really is just like his father."

Byron nodded.

"But if my daughter is with them, we must find them before Sarpene does."

"I think they will head back to your caves to look for us, Byron," Tenii said. "They do not know we've come here for them."

Byron nodded and looked back toward the queen, who was looking wide-eyed at Harrod.

Byron and Tenii watched as the queen and Harrod seemed to communicate with their eyes. After a few seconds, the queen sighed and nodded.

"What is it?" Tenii sputtered.

"We received reports a few days ago that Sarpene was gathering a force just outside of Kudosh." He sighed and hesitated. "There was also a report that even Sarpene himself might be there. That is why we took the boy in the first place."

"One of my dwarves should still be there, Your Majesty. He'll protect them until we can get there."

"Narl?" Tenii scoffed. "He'll probably send them away without telling them where we've gone."

"No," Byron shook his head. "He would not dare. He's old and stubborn, but he still has some sense of honor within him."

"Let's hope so," Tenii stated, unconvinced.

The queen contemplated silently for a moment, then looked toward Harrod again.

"Assemble the army. Get every elf who can carry a weapon ready. Let them know we leave at first light." Then she turned to Byron. "Can your dwarves travel quickly through the woods?"

"Faster than any elf can," he assured her.

Harrod rolled his eyes as he left.

"Good, can they be ready by first light?"

"To go after Sarpene? They could be ready in five minutes." Byron nodded again and took off to let the dwarves know what was going on.

The queen gave a worried look to Tenii.

"I hope this boy can live up to his royal name."

"There is no doubt, Your Majesty. There is no doubt."

25

Giant Trouble

"Dantin, Petra, wake up." Tierra's soft voice flowed through Dantin's head like a gentle brook upon rounded rocks. Dantin smiled in his sleep and began to stir. As his eyes opened, he spotted Tierra. Instantly his eyes dropped self-consciously and the smile disappeared.

"There is something going on at the castle, we must leave now," she urged, nudging Petra again.

As Petra began to stir, she threw some berries into Dantin's lap.

"Here, eat these."

Dantin examined them for a second and popped them into his mouth, too hungry and not yet awake enough to care what they were. The sweet flavor exploded in his mouth, waking him up faster than that nasty coffee Ms. Mullin used to drink.

"Wow," he said in wonder. "These are the most amazing berries I've ever had. It tastes like a mixture of strawberries, raspberries, and blueberries." It took only a few seconds for him to gorge the rest.

Tierra smiled, pleased with herself, and roughly shoved Petra one more time.

"Wake up!" she repeated for the fifth time.

"Ugh," Petra groaned, finally opening his eyes. He looked around and grumbled again. "You wake me up from a dream of meadows and flowers back into this place." He yawned and stood, stretching his hind legs.

"Eat these, quick. Then we must go."

Petra gulped them down and looked around.

"What's that noise?" he asked looking toward the castle.

"I don't know," Tierra answered. "But there are hundreds of elves around. We have to get out of here."

Tierra stuck her head through the bushes and called back.

"It's clear, let's go."

Dantin and Petra followed her through and took off away from the sounds of the castle. Energy surged through Dantin's body as they ran. He looked down at his arms and flexed them back and forth. He'd never felt this strong before. He could even see better, even in the almost pitch black of night. Smiling to himself, he leapt bushes and dodged trees that a few hours ago would have sent him sprawling. After they traveled for a while, he stopped in his place.

"Wait," he called.

Tierra stopped a few yards a head of him and Petra almost ran straight into his back.

"What is it?" Clearly annoyed, Tierra turned.

"Where exactly are we going?" Dantin asked.

Tierra looked around and shrugged her shoulders.

"How should I know? This is as far away from the castle as I've ever been." She looked around again. "I thought you knew where you were going."

"ME!" Dantin's voice began to rise. "How am I supposed to know where we are?"

"Great plan," she said, plopping down on a tree stump.

"What, you're blaming me?" he defended. "I just wanted to get away from *your* mother, you said that you—"

"Oh, would you two stop it!" Petra blurted in. "If you could have a conversation without arguing, maybe we'd get somewhere."

"Well, I got us out of the castle, the rest is up to you two."

Dantin's mouth opened to bicker, but Petra hushed him again.

"Why don't we go back to the dwarves' caves, they may be still there waiting for us."

Dantin cocked his head to the side and rubbed his chin.

"Yeah," he said thoughtfully. "That's what I was going to say."

"Sure." Petra rolled his eyes.

Dantin shot him another look and the princess jumped in before they could argue.

"Well, does anyone know how to get there?"

Dantin shrugged his shoulders and Petra stood tall.

"Of course I do," he chimed. "I remember every bump and bruise of it."

"Well, buddy," Dantin said, brightening again and placing his hand on the fawn's back. "I guess you're leading now."

Petra beamed and puffed out his chest. He looked around intently for a few seconds, then called out, "That way." He took off, and Tierra and Dantin shrugged their shoulders at each other before following.

Petra was relentless in his quest, running for hours on end with no rest. Every once in a while he'd stop, look side to side for a couple seconds. As Tierra and Dantin would catch up to him, each breathing heavily, he would nod to himself and take off again.

Dantin noticed the sky lighten a bit, bringing in the next day. Yet the air continued to grow thicker and was continually losing the sweetness he'd come to enjoy and becoming stale again. He looked up again, wondering if the sun was already up and if the sky would get any brighter. His question was answered the next time he looked up as he could see the sky getting darker.

"We're close," he huffed to Tierra.

"I hope so," she said, wrinkling her nose. "This rotten air is making me gag."

As if hearing their exchange, Petra stopped and leaned against a tree.

"Tired already?" Dantin teased breathlessly.

"No, we're here." The fawn looked as though he was about to pass out.

"Where?" Tierra looked around, seeing nothing out of the ordinary.

"There," Dantin called excitedly, pointing to the rock that hid the entrance to the dwarves' cave. "Great job, Petra!" He patted the wheezing fawn's back.

"Thanks," Petra blurted between coughs

"Where are these dwarves you've been talking about?" Tierra asked, following Dantin as he made his way to the large rock.

"They're probably inside the—"

"STOP!" The rough command froze them in their places. Dantin swallowed what felt like a golf ball and turned his head and found a figure emerging from the shadows, carrying a large axe. As the figure came closer, Dantin's smile returned.

"Narl, it's me, Dantin."

"What are you doing back here?" he grumbled, looking around. "Where are the others?"

"What do you mean? We just escaped. What about the others?"

"They-they came to rescue you."

Dantin looked toward Tierra and then Petra, both shrugged.

"When we left the castle we—"

"Wait!" Narl held up his hand and sniffed in the air. Motioning for them to duck down, Narl raised his axe and looked around, still sniffing the air.

—Hooowwwlll!

A wolf lunged out of nowhere at Narl's back. Tierra screamed and before Dantin could warn him, Narl spun cleanly, axe raised, and caught the wolf in midair, relieving him of his head. Spitting on the body of the slain beast, Narl yelled to the others.

"INSIDE, NOW!"

The three scrambled into the opening, followed by Narl, who struck another wolf on his way. As he turned to pull the door shut, another wolf appeared and chomped his wrist and tried to pull him back through.

"AHHHHHH!"

As another wolf appeared to help, Dantin reemerged and plunged his dagger into chest of the wolf chewing on Narl's arm. The wolf released and Narl slammed the door on the head of the second one. Securing the latch, he followed the others down the long stairs, clutching his injured arm close to his body.

"Here, let me look at that," Tierra cried, seeing the dwarf stumble into the wall. She ripped a long strip from her garments and wrapped it tightly around the wound.

"Can you still move your fingers?" she asked calmly.

The dwarf winced, but clenched his fist and released a couple times.

"Good," she comforted. "It's only a flesh wound."

"AAARRRGGGG!" Narl's eyes turned blood red and hate erupted across his face as he kicked at chairs and flipped a table. "I'm going to kill every last one of those cursed beasts!"

"NARL!" Dantin yelled. "Calm down! What are we going to do?"

The dwarf flipped another table and looked at the trio standing before him with eyes wider than softballs. Breathing heavily, some of the red drained from his eyes.

"Nothing," he spat. "We aren't going to do anything. We're safe for now, the wolves can't get in that door, but—"

The room trembled with an immense earthquake. Dirt from the ceiling fell all around and tables and cupboards fell upon each other.

"BUT WHAT?" Tierra screamed over the rumbling.

"But giants can!" he yelled, moving just before an enormous chunk of ceiling fell where he was standing. "This way."

He herded the group down a crumbling hallway into another room. Pushing them through, he went to a door on the other side of the room. He disappeared and reemerged with two axes.

"Here, this is better than that little dagger," he yelled throwing the axe to Dantin. He caught it, but almost fell to the floor in the process.

"Uh, I don't think this is going to work," Dantin called, barely able to lift the axe to his waist.

The dwarf sighed aloud and went back into the closet, coming out again with a short sword.

"Best I can do, kid," he yelled, throwing the weapon.

Dantin caught it cleanly, waived it around in his hand for a second and smiled.

"Now this is more like it."

Narl led them down another hallway as the current room began to crumble under the vibrations as well. They began to hear growls down the first hallway.

"In here," Narl herded them through another doorway and closed the door.

"Continue going down that hallway," Narl direct to Dantin. "When you get to the end, climb the stairs all the way to the top. At the end you'll find another exit the wolves may not know about. Once you're outside, run until you can't run anymore, and then run farther. When you get—"

"Wait," Dantin interrupted. "What about you? You're coming with us, right?"

Narl shook his head, grinned, and rubbed his injured wrist again.

"These wolves aren't taking my house without a fight."

Dantin looked to Petra and Tierra standing at the hallway waiting for him.

"Come on," Petra urged.

Looking back to Narl, Dantin gritted his teeth, looking back and forth again.

"GO!" the dwarf commanded, opening the door. "DOLO!" erupted from his lips and he disappeared into a flurry of growls and barks.

Dantin thought for another second, and then blurted out.

"Petra, Tierra, go where he said, I'm staying here."

"No way," Petra started, "I'm not going any—"

"Petra," Dantin called, pulling the fawn aside and whispering in his ear. "I need you to protect the princess. That's your new task. Keep her safe!"

Petra nodded solemnly.

"This is garbage!" Tierra complained. "I can fight too. There's no way I'm leaving you two to—"

Dantin pulled her aside next.

"Tierra," he whispered in her ear. "I need you to protect Petra, he's only a fawn, he can't fight off wolves."

"But—"

"Please?"

Tierra's eyes teared.

"Fine," she said, looking into Dantin's eyes.

"We'll meet up soon," Dantin nodded knowingly. "I promise. Now go!"

"Come, Princess," Petra insisted. "I'll keep you safe."

He and Dantin exchanged nods and the two disappeared.

"Here we go, Dantin," he said aloud to himself with a deep breath, opening the door.

He stepped over three dead wolves and found Narl surrounded. One wolf was in front of him, another behind, and a third above on the table. Each snarled as drool dripped from their fangs. Narl turned in circles, waiting for one to attack. Wasting no time, Dantin lunged at the wolf at the table, plunging his sword straight through him. Immediately, Narl spun a full circle, dropping the other two wolves in one motion.

"What are you doing here, I thought I told you to get out of here?" Narl barked, scanning the room and spitting on the wolves he killed.

"A simple thank you would have been fine," Dantin responded, standing up and remembering to wipe off his sword on his victim. "I wasn't just going to let you take on all these guys alone."

"Why risk your life for me?" Narl said. "You've sworn no loyalty to me."

"I don't know anything about loyalty, it just wouldn't be right," he stated. "You'd do the same for me."

Narl lowered his eyes for a second, but brought them back up to Dantin's.

"I would now," he said, bowing.

"Stop that," Dantin said, red faced. "How many more of these things are there?"

—BOOM!

Both nearly fell at the rumble.

"Oh yeah, I forgot about the giant," Dantin called, steadying himself against the wall.

"Well," Narl began, pulling himself up. "If it means anything, these were some of Sarpene's best wolves. They're part of Diffamo's gang, you can tell by the chains."

He reached down with his axe and pulled up a tag with a half-moon on it.

"Hey," Dantin laughed. "Dog tags."

"What?"

"Never mind. But if these are his best, then when do we get to face some of his worst?"

More growls from down the hallway answered his question. The two warriors hid on either side of the door and awaited their arrival. As they stood, weapons ready, Narl spoke again.

"Dantin," he said sheepishly. "I apologize. I guess you are as special as they say you are."

"What do you mean?" Dantin asked, taken aback.

"I'll explain later," Narl said, hearing the wolves get closer. "Right now, DOLO!"

Narl's axe took two more heads and Dantin's sword took another, knocking three more wolves to their backs in the process. Before the wolves could regain themselves, the two warriors were on them. Nodding to each other, they proceeded down the collapsed hallway, taking four more wolves out.

"How many is that anyway?" Dantin called, finishing off two more.

"That's six for you, and eleven for me," he called. "You're falling behind, Prince."

"What about the one at the entrance?"

"Alright, seven," he growled through his teeth, bringing his axe down again and again. He looked up with a smile. "But I'm up to fifteen now."

Dantin rejoined the dwarf as they entered the main room. The ceiling was completely gone, leaving only rubble beneath and trees towering above. They looked and saw the hole in the ground surrounded by snarling wolves.

"Where's the giant?" Dantin asked.

The room behind them crumbled as Dantin saw the world's most enormous foot crash through the ceiling.

"You asked," Narl said.

"What now?" Dantin yelled, waving the dust from his eyes. They stood in the small hallway between the two destroyed rooms.

"Make them come to us. You get that side, I'll get this one."

The two stood back to back, killing wolf after wolf.

"I lost count, what number are you on?"

"Forty," Narl yelled, bringing his axe down again. "I mean forty-one."

But the more wolves that fell, the more that came. Soon, Dantin looked upon six wolves, all drooling and ready to pounce. Narl looked upon the same, until two large feet slammed down into the room. They turned their heads to each other and exchanged looks of horror. Narl watched as large hand came toward them. Then Dantin watched two wolves lunge at the same time. He swung with all his might and knocked down one. He closed his eyes and awaited the second, but it never came. Slowly opening his eyes, he found it dead on the ground with an arrow through its chest. Three more arrows came and took out three more wolves. Dantin sliced and took out the last one and looked up to find Tierra, bow bent and releasing arrow after arrow.

"Narl," he yelled, reaching back and pulling the dwarf away by his collar as the giant grasped at air. "This way!"

As the two ran, Tierra picked off each wolf that followed. Scrambling over piles of dirt and rock, they made their way to the back of the caves and up the stairs they had sent the elf and fawn up. The giant, still confused by the missing dwarf, stood and scratched his head. They reached the foot of the tree where Tierra was posted and stopped, waiting for her to come down. The wolves didn't seem to be following.

"Good thing we didn't run, huh?" she smiled. "I told you I was good with a bow."

"Man, I'm glad to see you." Dantin reached out and hugged her. Coming to his senses, he quickly pulled away and looked around the sky, stopping his eyes on Narl. He was watching the wolves stand around the compound and the giant still standing within.

"Why aren't they coming after us?" Dantin asked.

"I don't know," Narl shook his head. "But I have a bad feel—"

—BOOM!

A flash of light hit Narl in the chest, throwing him back against a tree, where he fell and didn't move. Dantin raised his sword, and another flash knocked it from his hand. Tierra spotted where the flashes came from and let an arrow fly into the shadow, but it stopped in midair and dropped to the ground just before the shadow. From the shadow emerged a tall figure, cloaked in black. His face was covered with his hood as he slowly approached Dantin and Tierra. They stood in place, too scared to move. The hooded figure stopped five feet from them and began to laugh.

"So *this* is the savior of the kingdom," he howled, pulling down his hood to reveal a white, hairless head and beady red eyes. His grim smile produced sharpened black teeth and a long, forked tongue.

"Dantin," he hissed. "Come give your uncle a hug."

Dantin's eyes grew even wider.

"S-Sarpene," he muttered to himself.

"In the flesh," the sorcerer bowed. "And who might the lovely lady be?" Looking closer, he smiled again.

"Ah, you must be Sylvania's daughter. You're more stunning than your mother ever was. Your father must be—oh yeah, he must be—dead."

Tierra glared and tried to pull another arrow, but found them to be stuck in her quiver.

"Sorry, darling, I can't have you shooting me. But isn't this precious, young love at its finest. Tragic though," Sarpene shook his head and brought up a frown. "Dying, just as your love is blooming."

"Leave her out of it," Dantin barked, gathering every bit of courage he could.

"Ohhh, he speaks like his father too. I wonder if you'll beg and plead as your father did under torture."

Dantin grinded his teeth and balled his fists.

"Let's see, how's this going to go," the sorcerer said, rubbing his chin. "First I kill you and your little girlfriend. Then I finally get to kill your mother and father. Of course, not before I tell them how much pain and suffering you went through."

"MONSTER!" Dantin lunged and was knocked back with a wave of Sarpene's hand.

"I see you have your father's bravery too," he commented as Tierra helped Dantin to his feet. "Me, I prefer power to bravery. With power, you can destroy bravery."

Staggering to his feet, Dantin lunged again, with the same result.

"Perhaps I mistook bravery for stupidity."

Dantin tried to stand again, but his legs didn't hold the strength.

Tierra ran to his side and helped him sit up.

"Alright, I'm already growing tired of this," he declared, pulling a wand from his pocket.

"AUXILIUM MALEFACTOR FUNESTUS," he chanted, pointing the wand to the sky. A whirl of wind surrounded him and concentrated on the tip of the wand. The sorcerer's eyes began to glow and a red halo surrounded him. He brought the wand down and pointed it at Dantin.

"Valedicto, my prince."

26

Power vs. Bravery

"NOOOO!" Out of nowhere, Petra appeared, lunging at Sarpene. Before he could react, Petra chomped down on the wand.

"PETRA!" Dantin yelled as the fawn glowed bright red, showing his bones through his skin like an x-ray. The wand broke in two and the light vanished, dropping Petra to the ground. Dantin looked in horror as his friend lay lifelessly.

"Stupid deer," Sarpene spat, kicking the fallen fawn and gingerly rubbing his hand.

"Leave him alone!" Dantin cried, gathering the energy to stand again. Tierra held his arm and watched the sorcerer's face glow in anger.

"I guess I'll just have to kill you with my bare hands," Sarpene grinned, pulling up his sleeves. He turned to the wolves, hyenas, and giant.

"Come, my pets. Come partake in my glory."

Hundreds of creatures emerged from the compound and made a large circle around the group, biting and gnawing at each other, vying for the best position. The giant towered above them all, holding a large tree to his shoulder.

"Tonight, I take complete control of the kingdom," he bragged, approaching Dantin and Tierra.

Reaching out, he grabbed a hold of Tierra's shoulder.

"You first, my sweet," he grinned.

"Let me go," Tierra screamed, kicking and screaming, dropping her quiver to the ground.

"I said to leave her out of this!" Dantin growled, grabbing one of the loose arrows and stabbing it into the sorcerer's stomach.

Dropping Tierra, Sarpene staggered back a few steps and yanked out the arrow.

"Just like your father," he mumbled, examining the arrow. The yelping and barking surrounding the three fell silent, waiting for Sarpene to react.

"Kill them," he spat, backing away.

Immediately the pack sprung into action. Dantin hugged Tierra close and they closed their eyes and waited. But the teeth and claws never came. Instead, the air was filled with whistles and yelps. Dantin opened his eyes again and found the arrows flying from every direction and elves dropping from the trees upon fleeing creatures.

"DOLO!" echoed off every tree and was followed by swinging axes and more yelps from scattering wolves.

"DANTIN!" Tenii cried, racing and diving upon the two still clutching each other knocking all three down.

"Tenii," Dantin gasped. "Am I glad to see you. Where have you been?"

"Trying to save your scrawny behind. It looks like we we're just in time."

"That you were, my friend," Dantin cried, hugging the dwarf.

"Here," Tenii said, pushing Dantin away. "I brought you a present." From his hip, he produced Dantin's sword.

"Gladius," Dantin exclaimed. "I think I missed her more than I missed you, Tenii."

"I have no doubt," Tenii smiled.

Standing, Dantin watched the surrounding chaos. He helped Tierra to her feet and they watched as the wolves and hyenas fell all around and cries of "DOLO" accompanied every swing of a dwarf axe. He even found Byron, running down a fleeing wolf.

"What about the giant?" Tierra asked, watching a group of elves dodge his thundering club.

"What, Gigas?" Tenii replied confidently. "Why, he's the most cowardly giant in existence. Watch."

They watched as one group of elves took position and began flying arrows at the giant's knees.

"But those are no more than toothpicks to him," Dantin pointed out.

"Just watch," Tenii insisted.

Another group of elves swung from trees and fired upon the giant's eyes, forcing him to drop the club with a thunderous thud and cover his face. After a few more seconds, Gigas stomped away, blubbering loud enough to shake the trees.

Cheers came from the elves and they turned their attention to the remaining wolves.

"Come, my friend, how about we find Sarpene?" Tenii offered.

"You don't have to ask me twice," Dantin smiled, looking toward Tierra. But she was staring blankly at a hump on the ground.

"Dantin," she whispered, pointing. "Petra."

Dantin's heart sank at the sudden realization and he ran to his friend. Kneeling down, tears filled his eyes as he placed his hand on the fawn's side.

"Thank you, my friend. I'll miss—"

He stopped cold as he felt Petra's chest rise.

"He's breathing," he yelled. Tierra was immediately at his side.

"Go get Sarpene, I'll tend to him."

Placing his hand upon hers, Dantin nodded and took off into the darkness, followed by Tenii.

"Where could he be?" Dantin asked, scanning the area.

"Probably in the darkest hole, farthest away from the battle and any dang—"

A flash of light finished Tenii's sentences and sent him to the ground, clutching his stomach.

"Not quite that far," Sarpene hissed, emerging from a shadow again. "Moth, my staff."

The gnome appeared at the sorcerer's side and handed him a long staff.

Tenii groaned and struggled to sit up.

"You're getting soft, Sarpene," he winced. "In the old days, that blast would have killed me."

"I told you, sire," Moth blurted. "We're too far away from the castle to—"

"Shut up, you twit," Sarpene barked, slamming the staff into the gnome's face, dropping him to the ground.

"Don't worry, Tenii. This one will," he assured, raising his hand again.

"The heck it will!" Dantin yelled, charging the sorcerer. He brought the sword around in a wide slash, but Sarpene blocked it with one end of the staff and caught his side an instant later with the other, staggering him back.

"Not much of a swordsman, are you, Dantin?" Sarpene taunted, twirling the staff.

"We'll see," Dantin grimaced, holding his side. He took the stance Tenii taught him and motioned Sarpene to come forward with his free hand.

Sarpene sneered and attacked, bringing the staff down with all his might. Dantin coolly blocked the first blow and dodged the counterblow coming from beneath, spinning and swinging toward the sorcerer's midsection. Sarpene blocked the blow and countered with a shot at Dantin's head. Ducking and regaining his stance, Dantin awaited the next attack.

"I'm impressed," Sarpene nodded and attacked with a flurry of blows. Dantin spun, ducked, jumped and blocked everything Sarpene threw at him, counterattacking at every chance. The two backed away from each other and squared off again.

Sarpene breathed heavily and spun his staff.

"What's the matter, old man, a little kid's too much for you?" Dantin taunted.

Sarpene's eyes glowed red and he attacked with a fury, swinging wildly. Dantin saw his chance as Sarpene lunged with a blow to the head. Dantin easily dodged it and with all his might came down with a blow of his own, striking the center of the staff, breaking it in two. The sorcerer staggered back, just avoiding a slash aimed at his chin.

"Your father would be proud," he panted, twirling the sticks in each hand and regaining his stance. "I'll be sure to tell him that you were almost good enough to defeat me, just before I kill him."

"I'LL SHOW YOU ALMOST!" Dantin screamed, forgetting his stance and lunging at the sorcerer with a blow strong enough to chop down a tree. Without losing the smirk, Sarpene pushed the blow aside with one end of the broken staff, and Dantin watched with wide eyes as the other end seemed to move in slow motion, slamming into his chin. The world spun as his mouth exploded like a firecracker between his teeth, buckling his knees and sending him to his back

His smirk grew wider and Sarpene shook his head as he stood over him and stepped on Dantin's arm, bending down and prying the sword from his hand. Examining it closely, he raised his eyebrows.

"Gladius Aspectus, I haven't seen this sword since I was a child."

Still dazed, Dantin tried to shake the cobwebs from his head.

"It's quite fitting though," Sarpene continued. "I get to kill you with your father's sword." Bringing the sword up, he began to chant again. *"Auxilium Malefactor funestus."*

The red halo reappeared around the sorcerer as he brought the sword down to Dantin's chest with an evil roar that silenced the woods. Even the elves and dwarves stopped in mid-fight and watched in horror as the sorcerer brought the sword to the boy's chest with all his might. Dantin clenched his eyes and awaited the blow, but felt the blade bend against his chest and fall harmlessly to his side. Opening his eyes, he smiled at the blank expression of confusion across Sarpene's face.

"I love that sword," Dantin remarked, seeing his moment and kicking the sorcerer between the legs.

"ADAX CAPTUS ADFIRMO."

Reeling again, it was Sarpene's turn to look with horror as he saw Tenii's hand raised and a flash flew from his fingertips and into his chest, knocking his feet from underneath him as his shoulders and head hit the ground first.

Dantin scrambled to his feet, picked the sword back up and stood over the sorcerer as he grimaced and writhed in pain.

"Anger and hate," he gritted through his teeth. Watching as the blade hardened again, he glanced back and forth from the cowering sorcerer to the tip of the sword.

"Mercy," Sarpene whimpered, curling into a ball and rolling onto his side.

"I'd kill you now, but I don't think the sword would work for me either." He kicked the sorcerer in the side and spat on his face. Turning, he ran to Tenii's side.

"Finally a spell that worked," he teased.

"Yeah." Tenii coughed, wincing at the sudden movement. "I've been waiting a long time to use that one."

"Well, that was good timing." Dantin beamed. "What do you say we go check on the others? It sounds like most of the wolves have fled."

"That sounds good to me," Tenii answered, holding out his arm for the boy. Suddenly, Dantin was thrown forward by a great flash hitting his back. Grimacing and struggling to turn over, he found Sarpene hobbling closer.

"Stupid boy," he spat evily. "You're just as foolish as your father. You should have killed me when you had the chance."

The sorcerer closed his eyes and raised his broken staff above his head and began chanting again. Dantin's wide eyes met Tenii's for an instant before he closed them tightly.

"Auxilium Malefact—"

A whistle above his head interrupted the sorcerer's chant, followed by a loud grunt. Dantin opened one eye and saw Sarpene, still standing above him, but an arrow was sticking from his shoulder and blood was dripping from the corner of his mouth as his eyes looked upon Dantin with hatred and disbelief. A second whistle brought an arrow into his other shoulder. Dropping the staff, he looked blankly at the arrow, then back at Dantin. Gurgling curses, he staggered back a few steps, fell into the shadows and behind a tree. Turning, Dantin found Tierra on one knee, holding an empty bow.

"I guess I needed two shots," she smiled. Dantin winked at her and painfully pushed himself to his feet. The two met over Tenii and knelt.

"Wait," Tenii gasped. "Where's Sarpene?"

"Don't worry about him," Dantin smiled. "Tierra took care of that."

The princess blushed and looked away.

"No," Tenii gasped again, struggling to speak. "Make sure."

There was no mistaking the seriousness in Tenii's eyes. Dantin nodded and stood up, catching eyes with Tierra. The princess strung another arrow and Dantin raised his sword as they approached the spot where Sarpene fell. Carefully rounding the tree, Dantin found the ground empty.

"Where could—" Dantin began.

"Look!" Tierra pointed to two arrows lying on the ground. Bending and picking one up, Dantin found blood on the tip.

27

Home

Dantin awoke to a bright light shining in his face. He shielded his eyes and rolled over, and gingerly pushed himself to his feet.

"Arghhh," he groaned, finding the culprit. The sun peeked over the mountains in the distance, shining through the leafless trees. Stretching his arms to the cloudless blue sky, he groaned again, wondering how every muscle in his body could still be sore five days after the battle.

"Petra," he called. "Wake up and check out this sunrise."

"Go away!" the fawn grumbled, rolling over and wincing. "I can't move."

"Oh, get up, you big baby," Dantin insisted, nudging him with his foot. "When was the last time you saw one of these?"

"There'll be one tomorrow. Now leave me alone!"

Dantin shrugged and walked away, finding Tenii and Harrod sitting around a small fire. He sat down delicately on the log next to Tenii.

"Any word on Sarpene?" He grimaced.

"Nothing," Harrod answered.

"He probably slithered into a hole and was eaten by the other snakes," Tenii spat.

"Anything to eat?" Dantin grinned at the thought.

"Of course," Tenii smiled, handing him the food that looked like bark again.

"Let me guess," he shook his head and took the food. "Fly guts and caterpillar eyes."

"Don't ask," Tenii laughed as Dantin gobbled it down. "Floreus?"

"Of course," Dantin brightened, grabbing the bottle and gulping half of it down without breathing.

"Hey, save some for me," Harrod complained, pulling the bottle away.

—Errrrp.

"Sorry," Dantin laughed, grabbing his relieved stomach. "That snuck up on me."

"Well, that's not very princely," a voice called from behind him.

Dantin's face turned beet red as he turned and found Tierra approaching. She sat next to Harrod and took the bottle, finishing it with a single swig.

—Errrrrrrrrrp.

"Now that was impressive," Tenii howled, falling off the log as Tierra's face now turned red.

"Your mother would be proud." Harrod shook his head. "Where is she?"

"She's still sleeping in the tent, I didn't wake her."

The four sat quietly, watching the fire dance upon the small twigs, and Tenii produced another bottle of floreus.

"The trees are growing buds already," Dantin pointed out, looking up.

"This is the first sunlight they've seen in eleven years," Tenii said, looking at the massive trunks and thin branches swaying in the wind. "They are resilient."

"That they are," Harrod agreed, washing down some "bark" with the floreus. "Soon the birds will bring their songs back and the good creatures will come back to their homes."

Dantin smiled and nodded, hearing a bird in the distance begin to sing.

"So," Tenii began, looking at the boy, "are you ready for today?"

Dantin smiled timidly as a shiver ran up his back and raised the hairs on his neck.

"O-of course," he stuttered, dancing his eyes back and forth between the others around him. "Why wouldn't I be ready? I-I've been waiting for this my whole life."

Tenii smiled.

"Don't worry, my prince, I guarantee they are just as excited as you are."

Dantin forced a smile.

"It's too bad the dwarves couldn't be here with us," he blurted, quickly changing the subject.

"They couldn't move Narl yet, he's still recovering," Tenii said, slowly nodding his head. "It's a wonder he's still alive. He took quite a shot."

"Those dwarves are as resilient as the trees," Harrod said, taking another drink.

"That they are, my friend," Tenii agreed, then he looked toward Dantin. "Besides, the others are still scouring the woods for Sarpene and other wolves. After that, they won't be happy until they're back in the mountains rebuilding their homes."

Dantin nodded thoughtfully, recalling their sad parting. Byron had given him a special dagger that belonged to his father. The silver hilt was studded with gems and delicate carvings. He tried giving him his axe, but it was too heavy for Dantin to carry. He remembered shaking Narl's hand. The dwarf was weak, but his pride and strength shone through his eyes. Argus seemed the saddest to see them go. He kept on complaining how boring it was going to be with no more rescue missions or killing wolves.

"Nobody told me there was breakfast," Petra whined, hobbling over.

"Come, you lazy fawn," Dantin teased, putting his arm around him. "You can sit next to me."

"Thanks," Petra rolled his eyes. "I save your life twice, travel miles and miles into unknown danger to find you, and now I have to sit next to you."

The party laughed heartily at the fawn's complaints and Tenii gave him a handful of food, which he happily gobbled down.

"What a crew this is," Sylvania commented, joining the party. "Three elves, a halfling, a half-dwarf, half-wizard, and a fawn. I don't think Pangadesh has ever seen a stranger mixing."

She sat down on the log and put her arm around her daughter.

"So, are you two ready to get married yet?" she teased, looking back and forth at the looks of horror on both Dantin's and Tierra's faces.

"Married!" they cried in unison.

"Mother," Tierra cried. "I'm never going to marry *him*! He's rude, disgusting, and he smells like feet!"

"*I'm* rude," Dantin shrieked. "You're the prissiest girl I've ever met. I wouldn't marry you if you were the last girl alive."

The two bickered back and forth and Tenii turned to the queen.

"It sounds like they're married already." The rest of the party howled with laughter, receiving dirty looks from both of the children. As the laughter subsided, a pigeon flew in and landed on the queen's shoulder. They all watched as his beak squawked into her ear. She nodded, and he flew away.

"The party we sent ahead made it there safely and cleared out the castle. There should be no more danger in front of us. They also received a report on Sarpene."

"WHERE?" everybody gasped at once.

"One of our birds saw him traveling away from the castle, being dragged along by a gnome. We've already sent a party in the same direction, but who knows what they'll find."

"And my parents?" Dantin asked nervously.

The queen smiled and looked him in the eye.

"They are safe," she assured him. "They are weak, but they are being taken care of. The messenger said that they eagerly await our arrival."

Dantin sighed in relief and his eyes welled up.

"Let's go home," said Tenii, putting his arm around the boy.

The cheerful party traveled quickly through the woods toward the castle. Even Petra hobbled at a fast pace to keep up. Dantin stayed behind the group, walking alone and silently. The feelings going through him were very confusing. The simple thought of seeing his parents made him shake all over and he was having trouble catching his breath. He shook his head, trying to be happy and excited, but his stomach turned into knots and his mouth dried to the point where he couldn't speak. As they traveled, the magnificent trees became less dense, until he found himself entering a meadow. He jumped a small brook and looked up, finding himself staring at a castle twice as big as the elves'. Its glorious towers rose above everything, and though it looked dirty and unkempt, it was the most magnificent thing he'd ever seen. He never could have imagined anything so astonishing and beautiful. He stopped in his place as his heart beat louder than the running water of the brook.

"This, my prince, is your home," Tenii beamed, looking back and waving his arms in a circle.

Dantin stared, open mouthed, unable to move his feet.

"Come, your parents await."

Dantin willed his feet to move and he walked in a haze, unable to pull his eyes away from the castle for fear it might disappear. The party reached the steps, and Dantin recalled the apprehension he used to feel climbing the stairs into his old school. But these stairs were ten times as long, so the fear lasted longer as well. As they reached the doors, they were greeted by two elves standing guard.

"Your Highness," one said as both bowed. "The king and queen await you in the throne room.

The large doors creaked opened with an enormous sound that echoed throughout the empty hallway. Dantin felt a mixture of fresh and stale air blow against his face as he entered. He looked around at the dark, bare walls and the shiver returned in his spine. Each footstep echoed as they traveled down the long hallway to doors equally as great as the two leading outside. Dantin stared at hundreds of carvings covering the doors, each looking like the artist spent years creating.

"Are you ready?" Tenii turned, glowing with pride.

Dantin began to hyperventilate.

"N-n-no, I-I can't," he gasped, backing away from the doors. He leaned against the wall and used all his will just to not throw up.

Tenii sighed and nodded to two elves who pulled the doors open. With his head spinning, Dantin continued to stare at the wall. Tenii put his arm around him and led him into the room, but Dantin's eyes never left the floor. They stopped, and Tenii spoke slowly.

"Your Majesty," he pronounced with a clenching throat. "May I present Prince Dantin."

Dantin slowly looked up and found a skinny old man with a white beard longer than Tenii's holding himself up against an elf. He stood hand in hand with an elf more beautiful than Sylvania and Tierra put together, even through sunken cheeks and pale skin. Dantin looked at the man's blue eyes and saw more strength than he thought possible. The woman covered her mouth with her free hand and began to shake.

"Son?" the old man rasped, his eyes welling up with tears.

All the feeling left Dantin's body as he tore up the stairs, almost tackling the king and queen. The pair caught him between them and met, tangled in a three-way embrace. Dantin looked back and saw tears fall from Tenii's eyes and get lost in his scruffy beard as he hugged his mother and father tighter. No words were spoken as they stood weeping, together.

Printed in the United States
44363LVS00003B/151-255

9 781413 785531